Gray MacInnes Had Attended This Fundraiser For The Sole Purpose Of Meeting The Woman Who Haunted His Memories.

His donor's memories.

Though he couldn't imagine what he'd say if he did come face-to-face with Catherine Thorne.

Hello. I have your husband's heart and I think I remember you.

Right. She'd run screaming. But even if he never spoke to her, at least he'd finally be able to see how she matched up with the woman in his head.

She matched perfectly. He hadn't been able to take his eyes off her from the moment their gazes had met. He felt as if he knew her, could recall the scent and feel and even the unique taste that was Catherine.

Mike Thorne must have loved his wife deeply. And now Mike Thorne's heart beat in another man's chest.

His chest.

And he wanted Mike Thorne's wife with a desperate intensity he could hardly contain.

Dear Reader,

When it comes to passion, Silhouette Desire has exactly what you need. This month's offerings include Cindy Gerard's *The Librarian's Passionate Knight,* the next installment of DYNASTIES: THE BARONES. A naive librarian gets swept off her feet by a dashing Barone sibling—who could ask for anything more? But more we do have, with another story about attractive and wealthy men, from Anne Marie Winston. *Billionaire Bachelors: Gray* is a deeply compelling story about a man who gets a second chance at life—and maybe the love of a lifetime.

Sheri WhiteFeather is back this month with the final story in our LONE STAR COUNTRY CLUB trilogy. *The Heart of a Stranger* will leave you breathless when a man with a sordid past gets a chance for ultimate redemption. Launching a new series this month is Kathie DeNosky with *Lonetree Ranchers: Brant.* When a handsome rancher helps a damsel in distress, all his defenses come crashing down and the fun begins.

Silhouette Desire is pleased to welcome two brand-new authors. Nalini Singh's *Desert Warrior* is an intense, emotional read with an alpha hero to die for. And Anna DePalo's *Having the Tycoon's Baby*, part of our ongoing series THE BABY BANK, is a sexy romp about one woman's need for a child and the sexy man who grants her wish—but at a surprising price.

There's plenty of passion rising up here in Silhouette Desire this month. So dive right in and enjoy.

Melissa Jeglinski

Melissa Jeglinski
Senior Editor
Silhouette Desire

Please address questions and book requests to:
Silhouette Reader Service
U.S.: 3010 Walden Ave., P.O. Box 1325, Buffalo, NY 14269
Canadian: P.O. Box 609, Fort Erie, Ont. L2A 5X3

Billionaire Bachelors: Gray

ANNE MARIE WINSTON

Silhouette® Desire®

Published by Silhouette Books

America's Publisher of Contemporary Romance

SILHOUETTE BOOKS

ISBN 0-373-76526-6

BILLIONAIRE BACHELORS: GRAY

Visit Silhouette at www.eHarlequin.com

Printed in U.S.A.

Books by Anne Marie Winston

Silhouette Desire

Best Kept Secrets #742
Island Baby #770
Chance at a Lifetime #809
Unlikely Eden #827
Carolina on My Mind #845
Substitute Wife #863
Find Her, Keep Her #887
Rancher's Wife #936
Rancher's Baby #1031
Seducing the Proper Miss Miller #1155
*The Baby Consultant #1191
*Dedicated to Deirdre #1197
*The Bride Means Business #1204
Lovers' Reunion #1226
The Pregnant Princess #1268
Seduction, Cowboy Style #1287
Rancher's Proposition #1322
Tall, Dark & Western #1339
A Most Desirable M.D. #1371
Risqué Business #1407
Billionaire Bachelors: Ryan #1413
Billionaire Bachelors: Stone #1423
Billionaire Bachelors: Garrett #1440
Billionaire Bachelors: Gray #1526

*Butler County Brides

ANNE MARIE WINSTON

RITA® Award finalist and bestselling author Anne Marie
Winston loves babies she can give back when they cry,
animals in all shapes and sizes, and just about anything
that blooms. When she's not writing, she's managing a
house full of animals and teenagers, reading anything
she can find and trying *not* to eat chocolate. She will
dance at the slightest provocation and weeds her gardens
when she can't see the sun for the weeds anymore. You
can learn more about Anne Marie's novels by visiting her
Web site at www.annemariewinston.com.

Prologue

"**I**'m glad to hear you're doing so well, Mr. Mac-Innes." The doctor busied himself writing a prescription. "Twenty-four months post-transplant is a nice milestone. The heart appears to be functioning extremely well. Here's an additional order for your anti-rejection drugs. Any questions?"

Gray accepted the slip of paper the doctor handed to him. "Thank you." He massaged the area around the incision beneath which a donor's heart now beat in his chest. "Do you ever hear…do other organ recipients ever report…strange things after the transplant?"

The doctor stopped in the act of gathering Gray's file together and stared at him intently. "Strange things like what?"

Gray shrugged. He'd felt foolish even bringing up the topic. Now he felt even more idiotic. "Nothing, really. Just little things that I don't remember from before. Foods I didn't like before taste good now."

The doctor smiled, still eyeing him curiously. "You might want to talk to some other organ recipients. We have a support group affiliated with the hospital, you know." He hesitated. "There is a body of evidence, strictly from anecdotal reports by patients, that sometimes memories are transplanted along with an organ. It's called cellular memory. One patient found he craved fried chicken, for instance, and another enjoys beer when she never could stand it before."

But how many of them remember a face? A voice? How many of them have intimate memories of one specific woman that they've never met before? Aloud, he said, "Thanks. Maybe I'll look into that."

"They meet the third Tuesday of the month, I believe." The doctor glanced discreetly at his watch. "If that's all…?"

"Just one other thing. I'd really like to thank the family of the donor whose heart I received in person. I know it's against regulations—"

But the doctor was shaking his head before the last words hit the air. "You know the transplant program has strict confidentiality policies in place. What you could do is write a letter and let the transplant management program forward it for you. You may include your name and address. If the family wishes to receive your correspondence and initiate contact, they can do so.''

''I've already done that.'' He'd written a note barely a week after his transplant, although he hadn't given his name. At the time, he'd thought the family might prefer an anonymous contact. ''I just…would like to meet them. Or even see them from a distance.'' Maybe he'd write another letter and include his name.

The physician smiled with sympathy at Gray. ''I appreciate your need to express your thanks. But some families can't handle any reminders of what they lost. Having a person who now possesses one of their loved one's organs pop up out of the blue is too much for them to deal with. We try to protect their privacy.''

''I can understand that.'' Gray kept his voice calm and accepting, though inside he was shouting. *But I have to find out who this woman is who's invaded my head!* ''Thank you, anyway.''

''You're welcome. Keep up the good work. I don't know if I've ever seen a transplant patient in better shape at this stage.'' He paused. ''Of course, you were in better health—except for the accident trauma—than most people who spend time on the transplant list with preexisting medical conditions.''

Gray nodded. ''So far, I've felt terrific.'' *Except for the fact that I seem to have gotten some other guy's memories along with his heart.*

''Make sure you call me immediately if you run a fever or if there's anything unusual occurring. Unless you need to come in earlier, I'll see you at your next biopsy and checkup in six months.'' The doctor stood and held out his hand, grinning when Gray stood and took it in a grip that left no doubt about his recovered strength. ''Careful, I need those fingers.''

The doctor turned and left the room and Gray lifted his shirt from the hook on the wall where he'd hung it when the doctor had examined him. He realized he still held the prescription he'd been handed and he leaned forward to lay it on the counter while he dressed.

As he did so, his gaze caught sight of the file lying in plain sight on the counter. *His file!* He hesitated as ethics warred with his need to know, but after a moment, he reached out and flipped it open. A quick scan of the first few pages failed to yield the information he wanted, but at least he knew now that the donor heart had been flown in from Johns Hopkins in Baltimore, Maryland, to Temple in Philadelphia, where he'd received it.

A few moments later, he was still buttoning his cuffs when the doctor strode back in and picked up the file, shaking his head. ''I think I need some of those memory drugs everybody's taking these days,'' he said with a wry smile. ''Take care, Mr. MacInnes.''

One

"May I have this dance?"

Catherine Thorne turned slowly away from her mother-in-law, to whom she'd been speaking when the stranger interrupted them. Actually, she'd begun babbling to Patsy the moment the man had started across the floor so he probably knew he wasn't interrupting anything.

He'd been watching her all evening, though she had no idea who he was. Tickets for the charity ball to benefit the organ donation program had been available to the public.

"Thank you, but no. I, ah, I don't dance." She couldn't remember the last time she'd told a lie and the words stuck in her throat.

Beside her, Patsy Thorne chuckled. "That's ridiculous, Catherine.'' She turned to the tall stranger whose severely cut raven hair gleamed with blue-black highlights. ''Of course she dances. She loves to dance. Now go.'' She addressed her last words to Catherine with a gentle push.

Catherine forced a smile. She loved her mother-in-law, to whom she was still close despite the death of Catherine's husband, Mike, and she knew Patsy meant well. The older woman had told her many times that she was too young to hide herself away, that Mike would have wanted her to get out and find someone to share her life with...but Catherine still wished Patsy would quit trying to marry her off. In the past six months, she'd been introduced to more eligible bachelors than she could count.

Slowly, she placed her hand in the palm the man extended, lifting her gaze to meet his as the shock of his warm flesh closing around hers quickened her breath. ''Thank you. I...would be happy to...accept....''

He had the darkest, bluest eyes she'd ever seen, his gaze so deep and intense that she forgot what she'd been saying. He was looking at her almost searchingly, as he had been since the moment their eyes had connected across the room earlier in the evening. Who was he?

His hand was hard and firm around hers as he escorted her to the dance floor. When he turned and pulled her into his arms, she tensed for a second before she could prevent it. She hadn't danced, hadn't been held by a man in any way since Mike's death.

"I'm harmless," he said into her ear as he swept her into the rhythm of the waltz.

She searched his face. "Are you?"

His eyebrows, black and thick, rose and he grinned. "More or less. I'm Gray MacInnes."

"It's a pleasure to meet you, Mr. MacInnes," she responded formally, trying to ignore the way her stomach had fluttered up under her rib cage when he'd smiled. "I'm—"

"Catherine," he finished for her. "Catherine Thorne."

She gave him a small, cool smile, determined not to let him see how flustered she was by his nearness and the way he lingered over her name, drawing her first name out in a slow verbal caress. "You have me at a disadvantage, Mr. MacInnes. Have we met before?"

He shook his head. "No. But you were fairly easy to identify when I asked who the lovely creature in midnight blue was. You organized tonight's event, so nearly everyone knows you."

That was true. So why did she have the feeling there was something hidden, withheld behind his bland explanation?

"Are you from Baltimore, Mr. MacInnes?" She concentrated on social small talk, trying to ignore how hard and unyielding his muscles felt beneath the perfect cut of his tux.

"Please call me Gray. Originally, I'm from Philadelphia," he said. "But I moved to Baltimore a few weeks ago. Did you grow up here?"

"I did." She inclined her head. "In Columbia, outside the city."

He drew her into a tight spin, whirling her in a circle, and she felt dwarfed by his powerful frame. At five foot six, she had never felt especially small. Her husband Mike had been six feet tall but he'd possessed a slender, athletic build. Gray MacInnes had to be at least three inches taller than Mike and if he hadn't been a linebacker, he'd missed a golden opportunity.

He was astonishingly light on his feet for such a large man, moving her easily over the dance floor. She'd missed dancing so much.

"Penny for your thoughts." It was a low growl in her ear and a shiver chased itself down her spine.

She laughed, trying to dispel the intimacy that draped the two of them. "They aren't worth that much. I was thinking of how much I enjoy dancing."

"Then you should do it often."

"I'm a widow. I rarely have the opportunity these days." The words sounded so bald and starkly painful spoken aloud that she winced.

"I'm sorry for your loss. How long since your husband passed away?" Though his words were conventional, he seemed curiously unsurprised, unshocked by her revelation. Perhaps he'd also learned that when he'd learned her name.

"Two years," she said. "Longer than we'd been married."

His hand tightened briefly around hers. "Was it unexpected?"

"An auto accident. We were struck broadside by a truck."

His face pulled taut for a moment. "You were with him?"

She nodded. "But the bulk of the impact occurred on his side." Then she shook herself. "I'm sorry. This is hardly an appropriate conversation for a social function."

"It's all right." The strains of the waltz faded and a faster swing replaced it, but he still held her in his arms. "No children, I take it?"

"Oh, yes." She smiled easily, fully, as the thought of Michael always could make her do. "I have a son. He was born after his father's death. He's almost seventeen months old now."

Gray MacInnes went still; his arms were rigid around her. His blue eyes widened and if she hadn't known better, she'd have thought her words shocked him. "Did—did your husband know?"

"No. I—didn't find out until after he died."

They'd stopped dancing altogether now and she looked up at him in concern. "Mr. MacInnes? Are you all right?"

"I'm fine. Call me Gray." Those intense eyes were still fixed on her face. "That must have been difficult."

She was able to smile now, though the months of her pregnancy had been hellish in many ways as she'd mourned Mike and dealt with the fact that her child would grow up fatherless. "It was, but it was also an unbelievable gift."

"I can't even imagine what you must have gone through."

She made herself smile and take the words at face value. "Well, the pregnancy wasn't bad but I could have done without labor and delivery."

"I bet," he said, a grin lighting the intensity of his eyes. He relaxed again and his arms loosened. "Would you like to continue this set?"

She nodded and they stepped into the lively pattern of the swing but a part of her noticed that he seemed different. What had been going on in his mind in the past few moments? She couldn't shake the feeling that it had to do with their conversation about her son. Perhaps he'd suffered a recent loss. That might make him particularly sensitive to her experience.

Forget it, she admonished herself. *You haven't dealt with men socially in so long you've lost the knack.*

They danced the rest of the set. She knew she probably shouldn't encourage him by spending so much time with him, but she hadn't danced in so long, and Gray MacInnes was a wonderful dancer. He was nothing like her husband, and in fact was a better dancer than Mike had ever been, but there was something about the way he held her that made her feel comfortable and safe and warm inside. The way she'd felt in Mike's arms. It was a little disconcerting, and when she realized it, she leaned back from him and said, "Goodness! I'd better get back to the table. I feel guilty leaving poor Patsy all by herself."

As he took her back to the table where Patsy

waited, she saw that far from being alone, her mother-in-law had found one of her best friends. Two beautifully coiffed heads were bent close together, but they straightened and separated when they saw the younger people returning. Patsy's friend, a member of her bridge club, rose with a last smile and moved back to her own table.

Catherine performed the obligatory introductions and Gray seated her.

"Please join us," Patsy invited him. "Catherine and I spend far too much time in each other's company. A handsome gentleman is just what we need."

Gray chuckled, even white teeth flashing as he looked from the elegant silver-haired matron to Catherine. "Your time alone must be by choice. Two lovely ladies like you would have men swarming around if you permitted it."

Patsy laughed, a deep, throaty sound and Catherine realized with a shock that her mother-in-law was *flirting* with Gray MacInnes. "And he's charming, too. Catherine, perhaps you should keep this one."

"Perhaps he doesn't want to be kept," Catherine retorted. She was deeply uncomfortable with Patsy's unapologetic matchmaking.

"And perhaps he does." Gray's eyes were amused but there was a warmth in the sapphire depths that made her uncomfortable and she had to look away.

"What brings you to the gala this evening?" Patsy inquired, still smiling.

Gray shrugged his shoulders. "I'm not originally from the area. What better way to meet people than to attend such a worthwhile function? Heart transplants save a great many lives."

"True, although this isn't strictly a heart transplant fund-raiser," Patsy said. The warm smile faded and sadness filled her eyes.

"Of course not," he said quickly. "I merely meant—"

"But you're right. Heart transplants can be wonderful things."

Catherine sat as still as stone, wishing her companions would change the subject. The last thing in the world she wanted or needed to discuss was heart transplantation, for God's sake!

"I don't know if Catherine told you, but my son, her husband, is deceased." Patsy's voice was low.

"She mentioned it," Gray replied. "You have my sympathies."

The ghost of a smile touched Patsy's lips. "Thank you. My son's heart was donated." She gestured around the room. "This truly is a wonderful event, one at which we can help raise funds for organ donor awareness."

Gray swallowed, running a finger around the neck of his starched collar as if it were too tight. "I couldn't agree more."

"My one regret," she went on, "is that we've never met the person who received Mike's heart. I had so hoped…it would be so wonderful to see the face of the person who still carries a piece of my son with him."

Catherine made an impatient movement with her

hand, then quickly caught herself and folded both hands in her lap again. "There's no way we can do that, Patsy. You know the rules. Anonymity unless the recipient chooses to communicate."

Patsy nodded sadly. "I know." She glanced at Gray. "We did get an anonymous note from the man who got the heart, a lovely one, but I so wish he'd wanted to meet us."

Gray was nodding, his chiseled features sober. "Catherine doesn't share my desire to meet the organ recipient."

Gr-r-r-r. Catherine struggled briefly with a desire to strangle her mother-in-law, with whom she very rarely disagreed. "It's just…Mike is gone. And there's someone walking around out there with his heart, and it makes me feel a little…resentful. I know it's petty and mean but…" She tried to smile, to soften the words. "If it still works so well, why couldn't it be working in Mike? I'm sorry, Patsy, but I'd just as soon not meet the person who got Mike's heart."

"I'm sorry, too, dear." Patsy reached across and laid a hand over hers. "I didn't mean to be insensitive to your pain." She fixed a smile on her face and turned back to their companion. "Organ transplantation is a complicated business, in more ways than merely medically."

Gray MacInnes nodded. He was looking from one to the other of them, a troubled look in his blue eyes. "Complicated, indeed."

Catherine took pity on him. Clearly the thought of

transplant surgery wasn't a palatable one for him. "Did you move to Baltimore for business purposes, Gray?"

He turned to her with an undisguised relief that nearly made her smile and she relaxed a little. "Yes. I'm an architect. I plan to open a branch of my company here."

"Oh! You're *that* MacInnes," Patsy said, arching her eyebrows. She turned to Catherine. "Gray designed a new type of solar something-or-other..." She glanced at him for confirmation.

"Window," he supplied.

"And it's been a huge hit. I just read an article about you in the *Sun* last week. Apparently, your window is revolutionizing the solar building industry."

"Perhaps." He inclined his dark head, the very picture of humility. The image was hard to match to the self-confidence of the real man.

"Do you use your window in your designs?" Patsy asked.

He hesitated. "Not always. I'd like to be known for the quality of the overall design, not simply for designs that incorporate a particular feature."

"Have you built a stunning home here, and may we have a tour?" Patsy asked.

"Patsy!" Catherine was startled. Her mother-in-law usually was the epitome of correctness.

But Gray didn't seem to mind. He shook his head. "The sad truth, ladies, is that I am living in a very small town house in a very noisy area while my home is under construction. The contractor, however, informed me last week that there would be a delay so the short-term lease I envisioned is going to be a longer, uglier reality.''

"That's unfortunate,'' said Catherine.

"That's ridiculous,'' Patsy corrected. "You can't live like that.''

Gray smiled, shrugging. "I *can* but I don't have to like it.''

"You probably don't spend much time at home, though, if you're opening a new office,'' Catherine said.

"Actually, I do. I have an exceptionally competent executive office manager who is setting up the day-to-day details so that I can continue to design. My private office right now is in my home.''

"But it's very important to the creative process to have a living space in which you're comfortable,'' Patsy protested. "I was an artist until my hands got too bad to paint much—'' She held up her hands, showing him fingers gnarled by arthritis. "—so I know how difficult it can be.''

"Fortunately,'' Gray told her, "it's short-term. The office will be up and running within two months, and I can work there if need be until my house is finished.''

"But you can't continue to live in a place where you're uncomfortable—oh!'' Patsy pressed her hands to her breast. "I just had the most wonderful idea.''

The enthusiasm in her tone unsettled Catherine. "And what might that be?''

"Gray can have the guest house!''

"The guest house?" Catherine was appalled. "But...the water and electricity aren't even turned on." *And we can't afford to turn them on, either.* Besides, the guest cottage on the grounds of the large estate she shared with Patsy was located just out of sight of the main house. The mere thought of having this man in such close proximity caused a feeling akin to panic to flare to life in Catherine's breast.

"A minor detail. It's a perfect solution." Patsy turned to Gray. "It's a two-story, two-bedroom house with a complete kitchen, living room and dining room. Much larger, I'm sure, than your current situation and much quieter, as well. It would be perfect for you!"

Surely he would decline. Protest graciously and thank her profusely for the offer. And decline.

"That's too generous of you, Mrs. Thorne. I would be grateful to you forever." He paused. "Is it furnished?"

"No." Patsy cocked her head. "Is that a problem?"

"Not at all. I have some of my own furniture in my town home now." He raised his eyebrows. "If you're serious, I'd be delighted to accept."

Catherine stared at him. He wasn't supposed to say that!

"Wonderful." Patsy's tone indicated the matter was settled. "We'll have it cleaned tomorrow. You should be able to move in by the first of the week."

"What's the rent?"

Patsy waved a hand. "That's not necessary—"

"Yes," he said in a tone so positive that for once, Patsy didn't seem inclined to argue. "It is. I can't accept such a gift. And I'll have the utilities turned on. I couldn't possibly ask you to do that."

"Well, if you insist." The older woman's voice was slightly sulky. "We'll discuss it later and come to some mutually agreeable terms."

No! Catherine wanted to shout. *We will not!* But technically, the house belonged to Patsy and she could invite whomever she liked. And if she was determined to have this man become a tenant, then rent was most definitely necessary.

She stared at her mother-in-law, willing her to get the message she was trying to send with her eyes. What did they really know about Gray MacInnes? So Patsy had heard of him—so what? The fact that the man had patented an invention didn't necessarily mean he was a nice guy.

Gray said, "Since we've only just met, I believe it would be in order for me to offer you some references. I'll have them brought by on Monday."

It was as if he'd read her mind, or sensed her reservations. But he hadn't addressed them all. What about Michael? Had Patsy even given a thought to how a perfect stranger's close, constant presence might affect Catherine's son? Did Gray even like children? Patsy had promised him quiet and there were moments when Michael was anything but. She wasn't going to be forever trying to shush the child just because the neighbor needed peace to work.

She took a deep breath, willing herself to be calm.

Something about Mr. MacInnes unnerved her, though she couldn't put a finger on it. It was almost as if…as if his blue eyes saw through her polished facade to the far-less-confident woman beneath the gloss she cultivated as a shield. As if he *knew* her, somehow, though she was positive they'd never met before. He wasn't a man one would forget.

Apparently oblivious to Catherine's consternation, Gray reached across the table and gently took one of Patsy's misshapen hands, lifting it to his lips. ''You'll never know how much I appreciate this.''

He couldn't believe his luck.

As he directed the movers who were bringing in his furniture and his home drafting table the following week, Gray marveled at the good fortune that had brought him here.

He'd attended that fund-raiser for the sole purpose of meeting the woman in his dreams. Dreams? Hell, she wasn't in his dreams. She was in his *memories*. And he knew exactly where she came from.

She was Mike Thorne's widow. Catherine. He savored the syllables.

He hadn't seen the donor's name in his medical file, but he had seen the name of the Baltimore hospital from which the heart had come by helicopter. The organ would have had to have been freshly harvested since hearts were only viable for about six hours, so his donor must have died on the same date of his transplant somewhere in the Baltimore region. Once he'd figured that out, the rest was easy.

He'd gotten on the Internet and looked through the obituaries in the *Sun,* Baltimore's largest newspaper. As soon as he'd read about Mike Thorne's death in an auto accident, he'd known. Or almost as soon. He'd been skimming the article, pulse quickening with excitement as he realized that this man fit his profile. And then he'd read her name.

…survived by his wife, Catherine Shumaker Thorne…

And he'd known. *Catherine.* That was her name. Not Cate or Cat or Kitty, but Catherine.

The name had brought into focus the hazy image of a sweet smile and dark-lashed, soft blue eyes that had danced in his mind for months, and suddenly he'd been able to picture her face with sharp, vivid clarity, as clearly as if she'd been standing in front of him. Was she for real? Or was he going crazy?

He'd been wracking his brain for days trying to figure out a way to meet Catherine Thorne, to see if his waking dreams were more than simply that, when he'd read about the charity ball—though he couldn't imagine what he'd say if he did come face-to-face with her.

Hello. I have your husband's heart and I think I remember you.

Right. She'd run screaming. When he'd seen the information in the paper about the fund-raising gala for organ donation and read that she was on the organizing committee, he'd known she'd probably be there so he'd made plans to attend. Even if he never spoke to her, at least he'd finally be able to see how she matched up with the woman in his head.

Only his plan had had a flaw. She'd matched perfectly. Too perfectly, in fact. He hadn't been able to take his eyes off her from the moment their gazes had met across the crowded room. He felt as if he knew her, could recall the scent and feel and even the unique taste that was Catherine. A part of him wanted to snatch her up and keep her with him where she belonged, but she *didn't* belong to him at all.

He knew he'd made her uncomfortable and he was sorry for that. But not sorry enough to turn and walk away, so he'd approached her.

But, God, how was he supposed to handle this? Mike Thorne must have loved his wife deeply, with every cell in every tissue of his heart. And now Mike Thorne's heart beat in another man's chest.

His chest. And *he* wanted Mike Thorne's wife with a desperate intensity, made all the more painful by the knowledge that she didn't know, and never would. Never could, he thought, remembering her reaction to the thought of meeting the recipient of her husband's heart.

"Hel-lo-o!"

Gray turned his head in the direction of the voice and saw Patsy Thorne, Catherine's mother-in-law, waving vigorously from the verandah of the big brick house on the other side of the pool.

He waved back. "Hello, Mrs. Thorne."

"Call me Patsy! Care to come over for a bite of lunch? There's plenty."

He really shouldn't, he told himself. Even though the movers were finished and he'd just signed off on their work log, he should get into his new house and start getting settled. But…he might get the chance to see Catherine again. And if he were honest with himself, that wasn't something he was prepared to miss. "I'd love to."

He skirted the fenced pool area and walked up the curving flagstone path between the casually elegant gardens that flanked it on either side.

"Oh, how lovely," Patsy said as he approached. "Catherine's gone to a luncheon meeting and our housekeeper just put my grandson down for a nap, so I'm at loose ends. Come and entertain me, dear boy."

He grinned, despite the disappointment that swept through him when he learned that Catherine wouldn't be present. Patsy was irresistible. His own mother had passed away several years ago and though her quiet presence couldn't have been more different from Patsy's buoyant vivacity, they both shared a similar quality in that everyone around them was bathed in warmth and love. "I'd be delighted." He offered her his arm and let her precede him into the house.

"So what do you think of Catherine?" Patsy didn't beat around the bush as they settled down on the terrace with bowls of consommé and exquisitely prepared finger sandwiches of cucumber and egg salad. The housekeeper, Aline, hadn't turned a hair when Patsy had introduced them and told her Gray would be staying for lunch, and he made a mental note to compliment her on the food.

He smiled at Patsy as she returned the smile with a merry gleam in her eye. "Do you do this with all the men she meets?"

"Yes, and you're avoiding the question." Her eyes twinkled.

"Catherine is lovely to behold," he said, "although I'm not sure she is quite as radiant as you are in pink."

Patsy giggled, putting a hand to the bodice of the pale pink dress that looked like something from a turn-of-the-last-century garden party. "Flatterer."

"Merely honest." He toasted her with his water glass. "You have a beautiful residence here. I confess, I wasn't sure if I'd done the right thing in taking you up on your offer so quickly, but now that I'm here, you may have to pry me out again with a crowbar."

"It was my husband's family home." Patsy's eyes softened. "Giles passed away quite suddenly a few years ago."

A wave of pity swept him as he realized that she had outlived not just the man she had loved but their only child as well, and he put a hand over hers on the table. "I can tell from the look on your face that your marriage was happy. You must miss him very much."

"Every day," she said simply. "But I'm glad sometimes that he didn't have to go through losing our Mike."

"That must have been a terrible time," he said gently. *Mamie.* The word popped into his head without warning and he nearly blurted it out. Thank God he caught himself. Was Mamie a name her son had called her or was it just something his subconscious had seen fit to toss into the troubling mix his memories had become?

She nodded and her lips trembled. She pressed a napkin to them with age-spotted hands still elegantly manicured and waited for a moment, then looked at him again. ''It was the worst thing I've ever been through. I don't know what I would have done without Catherine.'' Then the sorrow in her eyes eased a little. ''When she was at the hospital being checked after the accident, we learned about her pregnancy. After the funeral and the shock of everything had begun to pass, we were so thankful that we at least had that last gift from Mike.''

''I bet your grandson is going to be spoiled silly.'' He winked at her, relieved when she smiled back and the heavy atmosphere lightened again. He desperately wanted to hear more about the child, to see him.

''Not if Catherine has anything to say about it.'' But there was no sting in the words and Patsy's smile was affectionate. ''She's a very good mother.''

''As good as Patsy is a Mamie.'' Catherine swept into the room with a smile and a kiss on the cheek for Patsy. For him, there was a single, very correct nod.

Mamie. So he wasn't going crazy after all. Although, as he looked at the woman before him, he felt like a werewolf in man form attempting not to give himself away by howling at the moon.

Two

Catherine was dressed in a slim-fitting pale blue summer suit and her fair hair was twisted into an intricate, shining knot at the back of her head. The severe hairstyle wouldn't flatter just any woman but Catherine wasn't just any woman. It emphasized the classic beauty of her delicate features, the sculpted bone of brow and cheek and jaw, the full, curving lips and her enormous blue eyes.

He was fascinated by those eyes. They weren't an ordinary dark blue like his own, but a lighter, softer shade that flashed with humor or temper and glowed with warmth when she was relaxed and happy. Despite the start they'd gotten on the heat of summer, her skin was milky white, satin dusted with rose across her cheekbones. He knew without touching her that it was as silky and tender all over, as smooth and sweet behind her knee as it was in the curve where her neck and shoulder met.

But that was impossible. He couldn't know that—and yet, he did, with a subtle sense of surety that was far more than wishful thinking. And his body knew it, too, he thought wryly as he shifted his legs beneath the table.

"Mamie is my nickname," Patsy said. "When Mike first began to babble, that's what stuck. He called me that all his life and now Michael does, too."

He nodded absently, still watching Catherine. "I know."

"You do?" Catherine's voice was as sharp as her eyes when she turned toward him. "How did you know that? You haven't even met Michael yet."

He shrugged, shaken by her perceptiveness as well as his own near-slip. He was going to have to be careful. Very, very careful, or she would figure out pretty quickly that something was funny. A sense of pride swelled within him. She'd always been one smart lady—

"Mr. MacInnes?" Her tone was questioning but as sharp as it had been before.

"I'm sorry," he said. "I was distracted."

"You said you knew we called Patsy Mamie?" It was a not-very-subtle interrogation.

"Perhaps he heard someone mention it at the ball, dear," Patsy said. "Heaven knows all I talk about is Michael. Gray probably overheard me telling someone an anecdote without even realizing he'd heard it." She smiled, anxiously looking from one to the other of them.

"You said it yourself, a few moments ago," he said to Catherine. "I guess I just assumed that was what your son calls Patsy."

"I see," she murmured. She still looked suspicious but he could see that she didn't want to upset her mother-in-law.

"How was your luncheon?" Patsy asked brightly.

Catherine's face lit up, as if she'd forgotten something for a moment. "Wonderful! I have some very exciting news." She unbuttoned the blue jacket and stripped it off, revealing a sleeveless ivory silk shell beneath it, neatly tucked into the waistband of the skirt. The silk was sheer enough that he could see the lacy swirls of some kind of slip thing beneath it, plunging low between her breasts. Yeow-za. He hoped she hadn't taken that off anywhere else today.

Hanging the jacket over the back of the chair, Catherine sank into the seat before Gray could rise to help her. "The museum board has offered me a position as executive director."

Patsy smiled vaguely. "That's lovely, dear." She turned to Gray. "Catherine volunteers her time with several organizations." He realized the older woman didn't understand what Catherine had just said.

"But this wouldn't be volunteer work," Catherine said. "As the executive director, I'll be salaried. I'll continue to be in charge of fund-raising." She sounded thrilled.

"Congratulations," he said. "What kind of duties will you have?"

"I'll be overseeing the staff, managing the budget and handling publicity, but largely I'll be concentrating on fund-raising."

"How does the museum raise money?" he asked.

"Federal, state and local funding," she said, and he got the impression she wasn't delighted with his participation in the conversation, although she didn't do anything that wasn't perfectly correct and ladylike. "Special campaigns, fund-raisers, bequests, income from trusts and endowments...like all nonprofits, the museum cobbles together all kinds of funding."

"In Philadelphia I sat on a couple of different boards," he said. "I'm familiar with what it takes to scrape together operating funds." He made himself a mental note to make an anonymous donation to the museum.

"Catherine?" Patsy's voice sounded troubled. "Do you mean you'll be *working?*"

"Yes." Catherine's voice was steady. "It's only part-time. And I can do some of the work from home while Michael naps in the afternoons, so I don't imagine it will be that big a problem. You and Aline shouldn't have to help with Michael any more than you already do."

"It's not that. But...I never worked." He realized Patsy Thorne wasn't being snobbish or denigrating; she honestly didn't understand why Catherine would want to work.

"It's really going to be like in-depth volunteer

work, Patsy," said Catherine patiently. "I promise it won't take time away from you or Michael or the other things I do."

The statement appeared to reassure her mother-in-law. "You know," she said, "since Gray is new to the area, you should take him to lunch sometime and tell him about all the local organizations that he might be interested in joining."

"What a good idea, Patsy." Catherine didn't sound as if it were a good idea at all.

"I'm free for lunch tomorrow." He didn't know what made him say it; perhaps it was a simple desire to see those blue eyes flash at him again instead of studiously ignoring him, as she'd been doing far too successfully.

"I'm sorry, I have plans for tomorrow," Catherine said. "Another time, perhaps."

"You have plans?" Patsy sounded dismayed. "Oh, dear, I didn't realize—I thought Tuesdays were your day at home. I promised Birdie I'd fill in with her bridge group."

"It's all right," Catherine said. "That was what I meant. Tuesday I spend the entire day with Michael."

He was amused to see a faint flush creeping up her cheeks as she wriggled out of the lie. "We'll do it another time." Her gaze met his again and he smiled blandly.

"Yes. Well." She rose and snatched her jacket from the chair. "I must go check on Michael. It was nice to see you again, Mr. MacInnes."

"Gray," he said, rising. "Call me Gray, remember?"

"Gray." She was halfway out the door and his name floated back as she whipped around and glared at him. "Goodbye."

"Goodness," Patsy murmured. "Catherine seems to be a bit…on edge this afternoon. I wonder if taking a job is such a good idea."

He could have told Patsy exactly why Catherine was on edge, but there was no sense in upsetting her. Catherine Thorne wasn't comfortable with him one little bit, though she was too well bred to say it outright. Sparks flew when those marvelous eyes of hers fastened on to him, and while he wasn't sure exactly what was happening, he was beginning to be fairly sure of one fact—Catherine appealed to him on every level there was. And not simply because he happened to inherit her husband's heart. It was *his* pulse that began to race even faster than was normal now when she walked into the room, *his* mouth that felt as dry as a cracker, *his* stomach that instantly tightened into a nearly painful knot of desire.

He was interested in her in a far more basic way than he'd anticipated, and he was almost as sure that she wasn't immune to him, either.

And that could be a problem, he admitted to himself as he recalled her reaction to her mother-in-law's comment about the donor on the first evening they'd met. Because he could never, ever tell her that he'd received her husband's heart.

* * *

Thank heavens Gray MacInnes had insisted on paying his own utility fees, Catherine thought as she breezed into her bedroom the following evening. She couldn't imagine trying to explain to Patsy that they simply didn't have the money to spare on generous gestures right now.

Quickly, she twisted up her hair with fingers made expert from years of practice and secured it with pins. She'd just finished feeding Michael his dinner and she had no time to lose. Walking toward the closet, she wondered what on earth her mother-in-law was up to…as if it weren't transparently obvious. Patsy had come home from the bridge game today and promptly walked along the winding path that led to the guest cottage. When she'd returned, she'd casually informed Catherine that Gray would be joining them for dinner that evening.

Dinner! She blew out an exasperated breath. She couldn't blame Patsy—her mother-in-law didn't begin to comprehend the financial concerns that hounded Catherine every day. To her, it was natural to extend their hospitality to their guest. Patsy had wanted Aline to run out for some far-too-expensive cuts of beef, but Catherine had talked her into serving Chicken Kiev, a dish for which she knew they already had the ingredients. And then there was the fact that this was a night when Michael normally ate dinner with them. Because Patsy had invited a guest, Catherine had fed him early and arranged with Aline to bathe him tonight instead of Friday, when Catherine often had dinner engagements and had to go out.

Dinner. She'd had to spend time she would rather have spent playing with Michael setting the table in the dining room, cutting flowers for the table and polishing silver that they rarely used anymore. Patsy, of course, would never have given those things a thought. Her mother-in-law had been born with the proverbial silver spoon in her mouth; household help took care of pesky details like work. She wasn't a thoughtless or unkind person. It was simply the way she'd been brought up—gracious, genteel, *pampered*. There were times—many more of them, recently—when Catherine thanked God for her own less-than-wealthy upbringing. If she hadn't had experience stretching pennies, who knew what might have happened to Patsy, Michael and her by now.

She was certain that Patsy wouldn't have known what to do when she discovered that Mike had invested almost everything they owned in some risky stock proposition that had gone sour, leaving them nearly insolvent. The only bright spot was that the house was debt-free, and if she could just keep up with living expenses and taxes, they might be able to keep it. Although she had yet to tell Patsy there was even a possibility that they could lose it.

She sighed. Dinner. With Gray MacInnes. It was bad enough that Patsy constantly set her up when they were in public, but now she was bringing a man into their *home*.

Mike had been gone for two years. She hadn't even thought of looking at another man for the first year-and-a-half. She'd been too busy grieving and then caring for her infant son. After she had realized what kind of shape their finances were in, she'd been completely immersed in trying to keep their ship afloat without unduly worrying Patsy, who had no head for business and seemed unable to grasp their accountant's concerns.

But a few months ago Patsy had begun to fret about Michael growing up in a household of women. She'd cooked up plot after plot with her bridge cronies, her golf partners and her luncheon pals to introduce Catherine to grandsons, nephews, godsons, next-door-neighbors, their lawyers and accountants and heaven only knew who else.

She'd managed to evade most of them, although there had been three blind dates, one of which was, unfortunately, too awful to be forgettable. And now this.

Yanking a black cocktail dress from the closet, she stepped into it. After sliding her feet into strappy black sandals, she stopped for a moment and drew in a deep breath. *Calm down, Catherine. Getting angry won't solve anything.*

Besides, she knew Patsy didn't mean to upset her. The older woman had welcomed her into the Thorne family so warmly that Catherine often felt as if Patsy were her own mother. Thinking of her mother, who had passed away when Catherine was born, invariably led to thoughts of her father, and she took another deep breath as tears stung her eyes.

He'd been a university librarian, often living in the world inside his head, but he'd loved Catherine

dearly, as she had him. His death during her senior
year of college had been devastating. The only thing
that had gotten her through it had been Mike, whom
she'd begun dating a few months earlier. It had
seemed natural to turn to him for help when she'd
discovered her father's gambling debts, and it had
seemed even more natural to accept his proposal a
few months later. Lord, she missed him still. They
hadn't even been married a year when he died.

Sighing again, she stopped to peer into the large
mirror in the hallway to be sure no trace of tears
marred the makeup she'd applied after her shower.
No tear tracks. Good. For some reason, she didn't
want to admit to any weakness in front of Gray.

As she descended the stairs, the front doorbell rang,
its tone deep and commanding. Aline, the housekeeper, bustled into view from the hallway and
crossed the foyer, and Catherine could hear her welcome the visitor. The voice that floated into the house
was instantly recognizable, and a shiver ran up her
spine, shaking her hand on the banister. What was it
about Gray that unnerved her so? He'd been polite
and friendly the night of the dinner-dance. She
couldn't find fault with his manners even if she tried.
He didn't ogle her or openly assess her figure like the
one jerk she'd gone out with. He was nice to Patsy,
listening attentively to her chatter as if he really were
interested. He should be the perfect man.

But…something bothered her. Something so
deeply instinctive she couldn't ignore it if she tried.
It was *not,* she was sure, the fact that he was incred-

ibly sexy and attractive, although she was well aware of him in that way.

Just then, the object of her worrisome thoughts stepped through the door and into the foyer. Aline closed the door behind him, said, "I'll tell Mrs. Thorne you're here. You go on into the drawing room," and rushed back the way she'd come. Catherine knew Michael would be toddling around on Aline's spotless kitchen floor looking for cabinets that didn't appear to have been securely relatched.

Gray began to cross the foyer. He stopped when he saw her halfway down the stairs. "Good evening," he said. "You look lovelier than ever tonight."

"Thank you." She inclined her head, trying to ignore the rush of pleasure his words brought.

He looked pretty darn fantastic himself, although she wasn't about to say so. He wore a black, silk short-sleeved shirt and matching black pants and the combination was both casually elegant and devastatingly attractive. His dark hair gleamed with raven highlights and his smile was a white slash in his face.

He waited silently as she descended the rest of the stairs and she was conscious of his eyes on her, though she didn't look at him again, instead giving unnecessary attention to carefully setting her feet on the treads of the steps.

"I brought you something." It wasn't until he spoke again that she realized he had kept one hand behind his back.

"I couldn't possibly accept a gift," she said.

He grinned. "A woman who doesn't love a surprise? Amazing.'' Then he brought his hand out from behind his back and there were two small packages clasped in his fingers. ''It's merely a token of my thanks,'' he told her, extending one toward her. ''One for you and one for Patsy, in appreciation for your generosity.''

She didn't know what to say. Not only had he personalized the moment, he'd just made her feel incredibly guilty for her churlish attitude. The guilt made her smile overly brilliant as she said, ''Well, in that case, I accept with alacrity.''

She reached out to take the small package from him, but he didn't release it immediately, and her fingers stilled as she glanced up at him.

He was staring at her mouth.

The moment hung, suspended like the dancing motes of dust in the sunshine that slanted across the parquet floor.

His face was taut, and as she stood, frozen, he lifted his gaze slowly until their eyes met again. His were dark and intense, *hungry,* and she sucked in a small breath of shock.

''Hello, Gray.'' Patsy's voice came from behind her, rich and musical, clearly delighted with his presence.

His eyes changed, bland distance replacing the desire, and she blinked as he dropped his hand and stepped back, leaving her holding the small package.

As he turned to greet Patsy, Catherine took several deep breaths, trying to still her quivering insides.

Dear God, there'd been enough heat in that look to melt her nylons.

"Patsy." Gray took the hands the older woman extended and kissed her cheek, then presented her with the gift remaining in his hand.

"A present? You shouldn't have." She flapped one hand at him as if dismissing the idea, but Catherine noticed she lifted the little box and shook it lightly beside her ear. "What would this be? And you have one, too? How lovely!" she said to Catherine. "Well, come and have a drink and we'll take turns opening them." Patsy gestured toward the drawing room he had yet to enter, then led the way into the room.

After one more frozen moment, Catherine followed her mother-in-law, feeling a little—no, a *lot*—like a leaf in the way of a steamroller.

Patsy immediately sent Gray to the bar, where he poured sherry for her, but Catherine refused any alcohol. "Just a glass of Perrier with lime, please." It felt so odd to have a man in the house again. She'd lived alone with Patsy for twice as long as she'd lived there with Mike, and sometimes she could barely remember what it had been like. That thought seemed sacrilegious, or traitorous—oh, this whole situation was impossible! She wanted to *scream,* but she took a seat on the striped silk chaise near the baby grand, tugging her skirt modestly down and crossing her ankles without really thinking about the actions.

She kept her gaze lowered as Gray walked across the subdued hues of the Middle Eastern patterned rug with her drink and another just like it for himself. His big hand dwarfed the glasses and she couldn't avoid brushing her fingers against his as she took her drink from him. The action, innocent as it was, seemed far too intimate to her superacute awareness of his every move.

"Come on, Catherine," Patsy said. She'd taken a seat on the deep burgundy sofa and was playfully waving her little package in the air. "We must open these!" She began to tear off the ribbon, but then she stopped, waiting for Catherine.

The last thing she wanted to do was open Gray's gift, but she knew her mother-in-law would never understand that. Reluctantly, she slipped the ribbon off her own small package and carefully pried open one end without tearing the paper.

"Catherine is one of those people who give gift-opening a bad name," Patsy informed Gray. "She can make a single package last a full half hour."

Gray smiled. "My mother was like that. And she saved the paper, too, to reuse. She actually ironed the stuff to get the creases out."

"My goodness! How industrious." Patsy uncovered a small gold box and paused expectantly, waiting for Catherine. Then they lifted the little box lids at the same time.

"Ohhh," Patsy said. "How utterly beautiful. And so delicate!" She held up a slim pin fashioned in the shape of a pale pink lily, enameled with an iridescent gloss that brought the tiny flower glowing to life. "I *adore* lilies. Thank you, Gray."

He inclined his head. "My pleasure, I assure you.

Your generous offer of living space was greatly appreciated. Now that I've seen it, I appreciate it even more.''

"What did you get, Catherine?" Patsy craned her neck.

"An iris," Catherine said. "My favorite flower." She looked across the glass coffee table at Gray. "And in my favorite shade, as well. Thank you very much." Her pin was beautifully wrought in a delicate pale blue exactly like her favorite shade of the pretty late-spring flower.

"You're very welcome." His eyes were warm and intent. "When I saw that one, I thought of you immediately."

Why did she have the feeling he meant that literally? Flustered, she glanced at her watch. "Goodness, Aline's probably ready to shoot us. We'd better head for the table."

"Where's your son?" Gray was frowning. "I assumed he'd be eating with us."

"I fed him earlier," she told him as he seated Patsy at the head of the table. "He usually eats around five."

"I should have known," Gray said. He was behind her now, pulling out her chair and when she sat, pushing it in beneath her. The action bent his head over the back of her chair and his breath ghosted across the back of her neck, making a shiver of reaction rush down her spine. "My receptionist back in Philadelphia has three- and five-year-old sons. They get exceedingly cranky if mealtime is delayed very long.'' He smiled as he took his seat.

The table had been set with salads and a cold consommé and Catherine ate quietly, letting Patsy's chatter fill the air during the first two courses. When everyone appeared to be finished, she excused herself and carried the dishes to the kitchen. With smooth, economical motions, she dished up the chicken breasts she'd made that afternoon, added asparagus tips covered with a Hollandaise sauce, new potatoes—

''May I help?''

Catherine's hand moved as she startled, and only Gray's quick reaction saved Patsy's lovely china from shattering on the tile floor. ''Goodness,'' she said. ''I wasn't expecting you to sneak up like that.''

''Sorry.'' His brows rose. ''I didn't mean to scare you. I just thought you could use some help.''

''Oh, no thank you. I've got it under control.''

''I can see that.'' His blue eyes were dark and a line appeared between his brows. ''Catherine—I'm sorry for putting you to all this trouble. When Patsy invited me, I just assumed you had staff to make and serve the meal. I wouldn't have—''

''It's not a problem,'' she said hastily. ''I just can't see the use of keeping extra help around when it's just Patsy, Michael, Aline and me. Most of the time, Aline and I handle the meals. If we're having a dinner party or something, of course we hire qualified help.''

''Well, I still appreciate all the trouble you've gone

to. I'd have been perfectly happy to eat in the kitchen.''

"Patsy would have been beyond horrified if I'd even mentioned feeding a guest in the kitchen." She smiled, sure he was only trying to put her at ease. Then she picked up two of the garnished plates, balanced the third on her forearm and nodded her head at the roll basket she'd just filled. "Since you're here, you could bring those in."

"Certainly." He took the rolls and held the swinging door between the kitchen and the dining room open for her, then waited until she'd set down all the plates so he could reseat her.

"Thank you," she said.

Every inch of her skin felt sensitized by his proximity and she jumped when his warm breath tickled the tender flesh of her exposed ear.

"My pleasure." His voice was deep and low, imbuing the conventional phrase with an intimacy that made thoughts fly instantly to slick bodies and silk sheets. Dear heaven, she could imagine all too well the pleasure she could find with him.

Subduing the images—and her racing pulse—took all the willpower within her.

Three

———

He *would* rather have eaten in the kitchen, Gray thought, surveying the beautifully laid table at which he'd just taken his place. No matter how many years it had been since the last time he'd had to worry about money, he still wasn't comfortable, deep down, with the trappings of exceptional wealth.

Oh, he'd gotten used to wearing cashmere sweaters. And he couldn't deny that he enjoyed driving sporty little cars, of which he had somehow acquired a few too many. Whirlpool tubs and the totally awesome exercise room in his Philly house were cool, too, as was being able to give however much monetary assistance struck his fancy to his favorite charities.

But household help? He doubted he'd ever take for granted the fact that other people cleaned his clothing and made his meals. His lawn got mowed by the same yard elves who kept his flowerbeds neat—for a tidy sum—and yet he still felt guilty that he hadn't mowed the damn grass himself. And he still shut off lights every time he left a room, turned off the water in the sink rather than letting it run while he brushed his teeth, and turned down the heat when he went away. He'd rather be boiled alive than hire a valet or a chauffeur as people expected him to do, and having little chocolate mints placed on the pillows of his freshly made bed every day, was frankly, embarrassing.

He was definitely more of a stainless steel than silver kind of guy.

Patsy and Catherine, on the other hand, were clearly precious metal. Highly polished, lovingly cared for, sterling quality. He wasn't sure yet if they were the ostentatious kind or quietly wealthy, but he doubted either of them knew a single thing about what it was like to leave the house in the morning worrying about whether your electricity would still be on when you got home.

It was an interesting meal. Patsy chattered nonstop to him and Catherine, sprinkling her conversation with stories about everything from her various civic groups and her golf game—which he gathered was dismal—to anecdotes about her grandson, which Gray drank in eagerly.

He learned that Michael had turned seventeen months old on the first of the month, that he spoke amazingly well for such a young child and that he hadn't walked until he was over a year, concerning both his mother and his grandmother.

"After all," Patsy said, "even though they assured us the baby wasn't harmed in the accident, we worried that some delayed effects might surface."

"*Patsy* worried," Catherine corrected. "From everything I read, he was right on the far edge of normal, particularly for little boys."

"At any rate, we're so thankful to have him," Patsy said. "He's brought life back into the house again. It was like a tomb after Mike was killed." Then, apparently realizing from the silence that followed that her choice of words had been less than wise, she said, "Well, you know what I mean."

He smiled, trying to help her past the awkward moment. "I imagine a baby lightens the heaviest heart."

Heart. Heart. Heart. The word echoed in his head and he wondered if he was the only one who immediately thought of organ donation and transplants.

"Are you originally from Philadelphia, Mr.— Gray?" It was the first time since the dance that Catherine had asked him a question. Even though he knew she'd done it largely to get past the silence that had fallen, her blue eyes were fixed on him with sincere interest.

"Yes."

"Oh!" Patsy was instantly intrigued. "Such a lovely, stately city. Is your family still there?"

He doubted she would have found the run-down neighborhood and modest little Cape Cod in which he'd grown up "lovely." But all he said was, "No.

I'm an only child and my mother passed away while I was in college.''

"And your father?"

"He was killed in an accident before I was born." And he might as well tell them the rest of it; the details of his early life inevitably came to light in the articles written about him. "He knew about me but he died before they could marry."

"Your poor mother." Patsy actually had tears of distress in her eyes. "To lose her young man like that. How awful. And in our day, of course, raising an illegitimate child carried a much greater stigma than it does today."

He could have kissed her. He should have known someone with a heart as soft as hers wouldn't be judgmental. He might have been honest, might have given her concrete examples of just how difficult it had been for both his mother and for himself, but a choking noise from Catherine's direction caught his attention.

Her cheeks were pink and she was staring at her mother-in-law, clearly scandalized. She was...she was upset on his behalf, he suddenly realized, because her mother-in-law had essentially just called him a bastard, even if she'd done it with the best of intentions. He was pleased that she was worried about his feelings, but he knew Patsy hadn't meant it the way it sounded. She just seemed not to hear her own words sometimes. He couldn't help grinning; he barely caught back the laugh that almost rumbled up. "I'm named for my father," he said to mask his amusement. "Gray was his last name."

Catherine cleared her throat. "So you and my son have something in common," she said. "You both were born posthumously and you're both named after your fathers."

He nodded, not sure where to go with the conversation.

"My parents are both gone, too," she went on in a quiet, well-modulated voice. "My mother died young, like your father, so I never knew her. I lost my father when I was in college. It was…difficult."

"You were close?"

She nodded, looking down at her fingers where she'd linked them together. "Very. I was devastated."

"But Mike took care of her," Patsy chirped. "They were married right after she graduated from college, and I got the most wonderful daughter-in-law on the face of the earth!"

Catherine smiled with wry affection as she regarded her ebullient mother-in-law. "I was equally lucky. Patsy's been like a mother to me."

"You know, Gray," Patsy said, her eyes on the bit of roll she was carefully buttering, "it seems silly for you to have a whole meal prepared just for yourself in the evenings. Why don't you join us on a daily basis?"

The suggestion startled him, coming out of the blue as it had. "I wouldn't want to impose," he said carefully, not looking at Catherine. He could just imagine what she was thinking right now.

"It's no imposition," Patsy said gaily. "In fact, I

think it would be a wonderful way to get Michael used to having a man in his life.''

Catherine's eyebrows rose. He gave her points for biting her tongue. ''Why does Michael need to get used to having a man in his life?'' she asked in a sweetly reasonable tone.

''Well, you know, dear, I'm sure you'll marry again one day,'' Patsy said.

He glanced back at Catherine, who just smiled and shook her head as she turned to him and said, ''Patsy won't rest until she's gotten me married off again.''

''Oh, pooh.'' Patsy waved a hand in the air. ''I just want what's best for both you and Michael.''

Had he ever heard anyone say, ''Oh, pooh,'' before? He couldn't help laughing this time. ''I imagine Catherine will work that out in her own good time,'' he said.

''Thank you.'' Catherine's voice held just a touch of exasperation.

''So, Gray, will you have dinner with us while you're here?'' Patsy asked. She was unshakeable, he realized. You might be able to distract her for a while, but you weren't going to get away with ignoring her.

''I'd love to join you on occasion,'' he temporized, not wanting Catherine to feel he was crowding her, ''but I'd better not plan on making it a daily event. Thank you for the offer, though.''

He wanted to see Catherine's son so badly he ached. But without making a pest of himself or conjuring up some artificial excuse she'd surely see through, he couldn't devise a way to get into the house to see Michael.

And so it was three more days before he saw the child of the man who'd given him his new heart. It also was the first time he'd seen Catherine since the evening Patsy had invited him to dinner.

He was in the spare bedroom he'd turned into his home office, halfheartedly working on a design for a sprawling, three-level home that a famous actor had asked him to design with a specific piece of property in western Colorado in mind. The plans were coming along beautifully and he was beginning to consider entering them in a prestigious architectural competition. *And not a solar window in sight,* he thought with guilty satisfaction.

While part of him was extremely pleased that the window design he'd created was functional and cost-efficient enough that it was making solar power a real possibility for the average homeowner, he was getting damn sick of every person who commissioned his work asking for four million of the stupid things scattered all through their houses.

He was roughing out the layout of a parlor/music room on the first floor when he heard a shrill voice through the open window. Drawn to the sound, he rose and walked across the room, pulling the curtain aside.

Catherine was walking along one of the flagstone paths that wound through the beautiful gardens. She wore slim khaki pants, sandals and a pale aqua camp shirt, and her blond hair was tied back in a long, loose ponytail rather than in the practical, severe upsweep he'd always seen before. At her side, holding on to her hand, toddled a sturdy little boy in jean overalls with a mass of white-blond curls.

Michael. Gray's hand tightened on the drape for a moment as a completely unexpected thrill of pride and pleasure rushed through him.

Almost instantly, he spun away from the window as shock replaced the first rush. What the hell was that? He'd read the theories about cellular memory in transplant cases, knew the anecdotal evidence that supported the phenomena he'd experienced...but what he'd just felt wasn't a memory. It was a—a *reaction.*

He let himself process that notion for a moment, but in the end he couldn't come up with any logical explanation. It had felt almost as if he'd absorbed some of Mike Thorne's spirit or something, when he'd received his heart. As if he really had experienced the thrill of seeing his own son for the first time. But...that couldn't be.

Could it?

The piercing giggle of a small child cut through his thoughts and he went with impulse, taking the stairs two at a time down to the first floor and opening his front door. "Hello, Catherine."

They were just turning on to an alternate path and she had to glance back over her shoulder. There was nothing flirtatious about it, but when their eyes met, Gray felt a zip and sizzle within him that he thought for a moment must have been heard in the air. Had she heard it? Felt it, too?

"Hello, Gray."

The sound of his name coming from her lips pleased him. But it was a distant recognition. All his attention had centered on the small person who had twisted around to stare at him.

"Hi," he said softly, hunkering down so that he was closer to the child's level. It was hard to speak; there was a funny constriction in his chest and he had to clear his throat. He didn't know why in hell he was feeling like this, but there was no denying that meeting Catherine's son was producing these overwhelming feelings inside him.

The little boy had turned clear around, wriggling free from his mother's hand though he moved partway behind her and peered out from around her khaki-clad leg. He regarded Gray solemnly, then a mischievous grin lightened his blue eyes. He looked up at his mother and demanded, "Who dat?"

"Mr. MacInnes," Catherine said. "He's going to be our neighbor for a little while."

"Mi-ter Mac," said the child with great satisfaction.

"MacInnes," Catherine repeated, but the little boy only grinned.

"Mac!"

Gray chuckled. "'Mac' will be fine," he told Catherine, though he never took his eyes from the child. "What's your name?"

The little boy's thumb crept into his mouth as

though pulled there by an invisible string. He grinned around it, but didn't speak.

"Can you tell Mr. MacInnes your name?" Catherine prompted.

"Mac!"

"Yes. Tell Mr. Mac your name."

"Mi-kuh."

"It's nice to meet you, Michael." Gray held out his hand. "May I shake your hand?"

The child shook his head vigorously, making the blond curls dance wildly. He took a step back behind the safety of his mother's leg again, although Gray noticed he was still grinning around that thumb.

"That's okay." Gray stood, brushing off the knees of his black slacks. He was standing in a bright patch of sunlight and he automatically moved into the shade. An increased risk of skin cancer was one of the side effects of the immunosuppressants he still took twice daily, and he had become cautious about limiting his exposure to sunlight. "Going for a walk?" he said to Catherine.

She nodded, absently putting one hand on her son's fair hair and ruffling the curls. "Michael loves to be outside. He'd spend all day every day digging in the dirt if I'd let him."

"Dig!" The little boy heard the one word that mattered. He grabbed his mother's hand and tugged with all his might. "Dig *now*."

Catherine laughed, waving her free hand in Gray's direction. "All right. Say goodbye to Mr. MacInnes."

"Bye." It was tossed over one shoulder as Michael

already was charging down the path, dragging his willing mother along in his wake.

Gray stood where he was, his eyes riveted to the woman and child until they disappeared around the shady curve farther along the path. She had the prettiest laugh…did she know how that laugh affected him?

He was standing beside the fire at a party with several friends, watching as a trio of young women entered the room. They stopped beside a gaily decorated Christmas tree, looking around as people do when they first enter a group, trying to catalog the crowd. Then the shortest girl spied one of the guys that she knew and made a beeline, the other two trailing in her wake. They performed introductions all around. One of his buddies said something stupid and the girls giggled. Usually he found giggling women annoying, but the one with the long blond hair had a pretty, silvery laugh that made him want to hear it again.

Catherine. Wasn't that her name? Without hesitation, he stepped forward. "Hello, Catherine. I'm Mike Thorne. May I get you a drink?"

She looked up at him, and he fell into the depths of eyes so blue and pure they simply swallowed him whole.

When his brain thawed and began to function again, the first thought that leaped into his head was: I'm going to marry her.

"Jesus." Gray put his hands to his head, shaken beyond belief. He realized he had sunk to his knees in the path although he didn't remember doing so. On the other hand, he remembered perfectly the scene that had just played itself out in his head...*even though it had never happened to him.*

He shook his head dazedly. He'd never considered himself possessed of an especially vivid imagination, but he'd never expected he'd need a heart transplant at the age of thirty, either.

This was nuts.

He climbed to his feet and for the second time, brushed at the knees of his pants. And then it occurred to him that there was a way to find out if he was dreaming or not.

"Hey, Catherine?" He went down the path before he could give himself time to think about why this was a bad idea.

She and Michael had walked out of the shadows of the big bushes and on to a velvety green lawn by the time he found them. The little boy headed for a sturdy, tot-size playset at the far end of the yard.

"Catherine?" he said again.

She turned, clearly surprised to see him. "Yes?"

He hesitated. "This sounds like a weird question but...how did you and your husband meet?"

Her smile faltered, uncertainty clouding her eyes. "That is an odd question."

"A bet with a friend," he improvised. He looked at the little boy rather than her, afraid she might see the need for her answer in his eyes. "I'm polling everyone I know."

"Oh." Her expression cleared and she smiled fully

again. "Well, in the interests of science…I was home during Christmas of my senior year at college and I went to a party with some friends. Mike was there. We hit it off right away." She laughed, and as it had before, the sound struck a chord deep inside, enchanting him so that he had a hard time focusing on her words. "Now Patsy is a completely different story. She and Mike's dad Giles were neighbors growing up. He pulled her hair and teased her unmercifully. She couldn't stand him."

"So how did they come to get married?" he asked. He wanted to keep her talking, to mask the shock that had rolled through him at her casual confirmation of what he'd already known.

"He was drafted," she said. "They exchanged letters and she swears she fell in love with him long-distance. They got married three days after he came home at the end of his first year."

"Ma-ma? Push?" Michael's shrill tones drifted toward them, and they both began to walk toward the child who was diligently trying to sling his short legs over the seat of a swing.

"I'm coming, Michael," she called.

Gray stood to one side as she lifted the child into a safety swing.

"No!" the little boy protested. "Big s'ing!"

"All right." Catherine pulled him out of the seat and settled him on her lap in one of the larger seats. "Mommy will swing with you." She held on to the child with one arm and gently began to move the swing with her feet.

"Mac push." Michael appeared to have definite ideas about this whole swing thing, Gray thought with amusement.

"Sure." He stepped behind the pair, cautioning Catherine, "Hang on to him."

"What are— Gray!" It was a shriek as he pulled the swing back toward him and then let go. They didn't really go very high, but Michael giggled and screamed.

"More!"

He obliged, pushing Catherine and the little boy back and forth for a few moments until Michael began to squirm. Catherine slowed the swing and set him down and he instantly trotted off toward the sandbox that was placed to one side of the play area.

As she straightened, an envelope that had been in the back pocket of her casual slacks slipped free and fell to the ground. Small pieces, many of them slick magazine-style paper, scattered and she bent to gather them.

Gray helped her, realizing as he did so that he was picking up already-clipped coupons. He smiled. Coupons reminded him instantly of his mother.

"You don't have to help—" she began, but when he held out the fistful of coupons he'd retrieved from the light breeze, she said, "Thank you." Her cheeks were pink, and as she stuffed them back into the envelope, she said, "For the senior center."

"Ah." He watched as she stuffed everything back into the envelope. "My mother was the coupon queen. I never saw anyone stretch a budget as well as that woman did.''

The edges of her lips softened from the firm line into which she'd drawn them. ''Coupons can be very helpful to someone on a limited income.''

He nodded. ''It's thoughtful of you to do that.'' She hesitated, and he wondered what she had been about to say, but then she shifted her attention to the little boy who had plopped down in the middle of the pile of sand. ''Michael! We don't eat sand.''

Gray chuckled as the child removed a shovel from his mouth with a distinctly guilty look. ''Apparently, some of us do.''

She laughed, too. ''Some of us more than others,'' she said dryly as she moved forward to halt her son's snacking. ''I have to watch him like a hawk. He wants to taste everything.''

''I'll keep that in mind in case I'm ever in a position to discourage a taste test,'' he said.

Catherine had settled herself on the edge of the sandbox and was helping her son fill a big bucket, scoop by scoop. She smiled up at him, and his breath caught like a fist in his chest. God, she was so lovely. ''Thanks,'' she said. ''Don't let us keep you from working. I'll try to keep him quiet.''

''Oh, you won't bother me.'' Ha. What a lie.

''Mac!'' Michael was pointing up at him, and he couldn't resist hunkering down beside the sandbox and grinning at the little boy.

''Hey, buddy, what's up?''

''Mac.'' Michael thrust one of the sturdy sand

scoops at him. His vocabulary might be limited, but his meaning was certainly clear.

"All right." Gray accepted the scoop. "You want me to build you a castle?"

The little boy's eyes lit up and his tiny, perfect teeth glistened as he grinned. "Uh-huh!"

The sand was cool, shaded by the long shadow of several trees that overlooked the little play area, and faintly damp from a late-afternoon shower yesterday. Perfect for molding and holding a shape.

Gray grabbed a bucket and started filling it, and Michael immediately joined in, patting the top industriously when the bucket was full. Gray turned it upside down and tapped carefully, and when he lifted it off, a perfect round tower stood on the level spot Catherine had made.

They did it several more times, making a fort of sorts, and then Gray set about fashioning walls between the towers. Michael squealed and filled the bucket again, his small, dimpled hands patting the top down.

Gray had almost finished scalloping a design along the uppermost edge of one of the towers when he noticed that Michael had lost interest in the project and was busily loading sand into a red truck.

He sat back on his heels, rubbing the sand off his hands and brushing at his clothing, now liberally sprinkled with white grains of sand. Looking over the little boy's head at Catherine, he said, "I guess the construction crew's finished for the day."

She smiled fondly, looking at her son. "His powers

of concentration leave something to be desired. From everything I've read, short attention span comes with the age—Michael!'' Her voice rose to an urgent pitch. ''Don't—''

Gray turned his head just in time to see the child plop his bulky bottom squarely into the middle of the castle they'd built.

''—sit on that,'' she finished in a resigned tone.

Gray watched intently as Catherine plucked the little guy out of the sand and dusted off his minute overalls. He'd never spent much time around toddlers—or kids of any age, for that matter—but he figured Michael's behavior was probably pretty typical. The little guy was clearly tickled pink with himself, squealing and giggling. He squirmed away from his mother's ministrations. The minute she let him go, he was off across the grass on another adventure.

Catherine's eyes met Gray's over the remains of the sandcastle. They were brimming with mirth and he felt a bubble of amusement rise in his own chest. An instant later, she burst into peals of silvery laughter. Unable to resist, he began to chuckle himself.

She laughed until the tears ran. ''The look on your face was priceless,'' she gasped, holding her stomach. ''Your masterpiece, smashed flat by a smelly diaper.''

''It was worth it,'' he said when he could talk again. ''Did you see how pleased he was with himself?''

Catherine nodded, still chuckling. ''Little stinker. Whenever I see that gleam in his eye, I know he's cooking up something ornery.''

"I'll have to remember that."

Her laughter faded away and there was a companionable silence between them as they watched the tot amble across the yard, babbling to himself in some incomprehensible language. She sighed. "He's such fun. It breaks my heart that he's going to grow up without knowing his father, and that Mike will never share all these precious moments with me." She wasn't tearful, just sadly reflective.

Gray nearly bit his tongue, so strong was the impulse to blurt out the truth to her. But…what *was* the truth, he asked himself? She'd think he was a nutcase, and maybe he was. Maybe all this was in his head.

Yeah. You just happen to know all kinds of intimate details about Catherine's life with her deceased husband. Details you couldn't possibly know unless you'd known the family before your transplant.

His heart transplant. It all came back to one split second on a rugby field, one flying kick that had struck him squarely in the chest, doing unimaginable damage and sending him to the hospital in full cardiac arrest, broken bones tearing jagged rips into the vital, life-giving organ, damaging it beyond any hope of repair. One moment, he'd been the picture of health. The next, he'd rocketed to the top of the transplant list, with little hope of a match occurring in time to replace his failing heart.

What cosmic stroke of fate had ended Mike Thorne's life in Baltimore, less than an hour by air from the hospital in which he, Gray, lay dying? And by what even less likely chance had they been a perfect match?

It was almost enough to make him believe in predestination. Fate. Whatever. All he really knew was that he wanted Catherine Thorne, wanted her more than he'd ever dreamed he could want a woman.

And he couldn't have her. There was simply no way he could ever hope to explain why he'd kept his transplant a secret from her, much less the rest of it.

No way at all.

Four

For the senior center. Catherine snorted inelegantly as she gently misted the climbing rose on the trellis at the back of the house with aphid spray later that same evening. It hadn't been a lie…exactly. She did give coupons to the senior center, after she'd gone through them to determine which ones she couldn't use herself.

She felt her cheeks heat as remembered embarrassment returned to haunt her. He'd been smiling, laughing at her, she'd thought at first as she'd scrambled to gather up the coupons before he could see them. But then he'd mentioned his mother and she'd realized his smile was one of reminiscence. Had his childhood been one of counting pennies, too? If it had been, he didn't seem to have been negatively affected by it.

Neither had she, she supposed. Her father had loved her deeply, and despite his ineptitude at managing money, she'd loved him as well. Still, her growing-up years had been a recurring episode of coming home from school to find the electricity had been cut off or the telephone service had been suspended. By the time she was thirteen she'd begun to open the mail and remind her father to pay the bills promptly. She'd become quite good at making the small amounts he remembered to hand her stretch to a week's worth of groceries. It wasn't until after his death when she'd gone through his things that she'd realized all the little ticketlike papers she'd found were betting stubs from the track, with the names of the horses, the odds and his bets listed beside them. She'd never really questioned their lack of funds, assuming that his salary as a university librarian had been less than adequate. It had been a shock to see proof of a gambling addiction, though it hadn't dimmed the love she'd felt.

She'd attended Smith College on a scholarship, coming home just often enough to be sure her father didn't get his water or lights cut off again. Smith was an elite school with many of the students coming from the old-money East Coast's most influential families. Some of them had been pleasant, but a lot of them had been exceedingly conscious of their own status compared to that of the rest of the student body. She had found it difficult to overcome the stigma of being a scholarship student who also pursued a work-study program to make ends meet.

After she'd married, money had no longer been a concern. But she would never forget the humiliation she'd felt when she'd lacked the funds to join the prestigious sorority into which she'd been invited. Or when she'd had to take an extra baby-sitting job to pay for her books, when she'd worn the same clothes for four years while girls around her changed wardrobes with the change of seasons. She'd told herself those things didn't matter, that she didn't want to be as shallow as her college acquaintances, that there were many things in life more important than money.

And there were. Mike's death had vividly illustrated the insignificance of money compared to the loss of a loved one.

But even when Mike had been living and money hadn't been a problem, she'd never been frivolous. Good items of clothing, not too flashy or trendy, made wardrobe staples for years, and she wasn't about to change her habits just because her financial situation had changed.

It was an attitude for which she was thankful as she'd realized the extent of Mike's financial straits after his death.

"Catherine?"

She came back to the present with a jolt to find Gray standing on the path staring at her curiously. "Oh, hello. Sorry," she said hastily, ignoring the way her pulse kicked into a more rapid gear. "Daydreaming."

"Where's your sidekick?" he asked, looking around.

She smiled, tapping the face of her watch. "It's eight-thirty. Michael's usually in bed by eight. I just wanted to give these roses a shot of spray to keep the bugs from ruining them."

"They're beautiful," he said. "I noticed you have a lot of roses. They're a good bit of work, aren't they?"

"Yes." She laid down the spray and picked up pruning shears, moving to a lovely apricot specimen on the other side of the path. "But I don't mind. Gardening is therapeutic for me. It only takes a few hours a week to keep things in good shape."

"I assumed you had someone to take care of this," he said, sounding surprised. "You do *all* the work yourself?"

"Almost all." She kept her gaze on the rose she was pruning, although she could feel heat stealing into her cheeks. Thankfully, it was dusk already and he probably couldn't see her face well. "It's not that much of a job. The landscaping really doesn't take much work if I give it a little time each week and I don't do the mowing myself."

He shook his head. "You're an amazing woman, do you know that?"

She shook her head. "No, I'm not." She set the pruning shears back in the basket she carried.

"According to Patsy, you're a combination of a superhero and June Cleaver all rolled into one."

That made her laugh as she got to her feet. "That's a scary notion."

"She's determined to get you into circulation again," he said. He'd stepped forward to offer a hand when she'd risen but she'd pretended she hadn't noticed. Touching Gray wouldn't be a smart thing to do, not when the man's mere presence in her vicinity made her whole body feel as if it were loaded with fizzy champagne bubbles. "She thinks you're far too serious for a young woman."

Abruptly, she was angry. Far more angry than Gray's words warranted, and she had to concentrate on beating back the unreasonable fury that rose. "If I'm serious, it's because I have a family to take care of and a house to run," she said sharply. "Patsy doesn't seem to understand that *someone* in this family has to be responsible."

There was a dead silence in the dark garden. Guilt gnawed a hole through her annoyance and left shame in its wake. Patsy loved her, depended on her. It wasn't Patsy's fault she'd never had to think about money a day in her life. And she should be grateful that her mother-in-law worried about her happiness. If she were going to assign blame for their present circumstances—*no!* That wasn't a road she could allow her thoughts to travel, and she worked at calming the anger still simmering inside her.

"I apologize," she said quietly.

Gray's head swung from contemplation of the garden, and even in the semidusk she could feel the intensity of his eyes. "For what?"

"You know for what," she said in a weary tone. That was how she felt. Weary. Tired of trying to out-smart Patsy's maneuvers. "I am well aware that at times I've been less than gracious in my welcome to our home. It's just that…" Belatedly, she realized she was on the verge of confiding in a man she barely knew and she shut her mouth so quickly she nearly bit her tongue.

"Just what?" His voice was a soothing baritone in the gloaming.

She sighed. "Nothing."

Gray was silent. She turned and looked away, out over the garden. Climbing the trellis that framed the gate to the swimming pool, the flowers of a white clematis glowed in the dusk as if they were lit from within.

"Just what?" he asked again. At the same instant, two big hands came down on her shoulders and began to massage.

Catherine practically leaped off the path. She'd never even heard him move. Automatically she began to move away but his hands kept up the soothing rhythm, his thumbs rubbing firm circles directly over knots at the base of her neck she hadn't even realized she had.

It was the first time he'd touched her since they'd danced, and here in the ever-deepening darkness it felt terribly intimate.

"Hold still," he said. "Your shoulders feel like they've been set in concrete."

"T-t-tension." Her teeth were chattering and her

nerves felt even more tightly stretched than ever. She stood silently, rigid beneath his hands, hearing the slide of fabric beneath his fingers. Above her, his breathing sounded loud in the quiet of the night around them.

As he ran his thumbs beneath her hair, he said, "What's got you so uptight?"

"You."

His fingers stopped abruptly. Silence.

The instant she blurted out the word she was sorry. What was she thinking? He was a guest of her family, nothing more, nothing less. "I meant—"

"Shhh." His hands left her shoulders. Turning her gently to face him, he laid a finger against her lips; the other hand clasped her neck, long fingers sliding up into her hair just behind her ear. "I know what you meant. You make me pretty damn tense, too, lady."

She lifted her own hands and wrapped them around his thick wrists. To pull him away? She didn't know anymore.

"Catherine." His voice was low and rough, filled with need. "I have to kiss you."

It was an odd way to put it, but she knew exactly what he meant. As he bent toward her, she lifted her face to his as if compelled to do so, her hands clutching his wrists as if they were her only lifelines in a wild and storm-tossed sea. His arms felt thick and muscled beneath her fingers, the hair rough and crisp and he smelled enticingly masculine, a combination of both the cologne he wore and his own completely male scent.

The moment his lips touched hers, she knew she'd been lying to herself. He was far, far more than simply a guest of Patsy's, a tenant renting their cottage. He was danger. He was desire. He was everything she'd once had, everything that had been brutally torn from her in one fatal instant, everything she'd been missing for the past two years. And if she were honest with herself, he was much more.

He was unfamiliar and yet familiar, tall and strange and yet somehow she felt as though she'd been in his arms before. His embrace felt familiar, even though his body was bigger and harder than her husband's had been, surrounding her with heat as he pulled her more securely against him.

He held her against him with one hand at her back while the other slipped up to cradle her head, cupping her scalp. The way he handled her felt easy and comfortable, as if they'd stood like this a hundred times and she felt herself relax into the moment.

His mouth was on hers, shaping and molding, and she clung to him blindly, her body thrilling to life beneath his touch. It had been so long since she'd known this, so long…. She couldn't prevent the small sound of delight that rose in her throat and the part of her that wasn't fully engaged in responding to his all-consuming kisses was briefly amazed at herself.

Lovemaking with her husband had been enjoyable, fun. But never like this, crashing over her like a tidal wave, robbing her of control and turning her into a needy mass of nerve endings begging to be stimulated.

His tongue brushed over the sealed line of her lips and she jolted in his arms. The small touch sent flares of sensation rocketing straight through her body, contracting her nipples and her womb instantly. Her knees wobbled and she felt him gather her more strongly against him, pressing her into full, firm contact with the ridge of male arousal surging against her soft stomach. She moaned again as her breath rushed out, and opened her mouth beneath his. He took immediate advantage, sliding his tongue inside her lips and probing the sensitive interior, finding and twining around hers in an erotic dance that drew her into a game of shockingly abandoned hide-and-seek.

She couldn't be still, couldn't stop her body from rocking against his, couldn't prevent herself from raising one leg and twining it around the back of his calf and tugging him closer. The action spread her thighs and pulled his hard body into closer contact with the soft, throbbing center of her and she moaned into his mouth.

His hands slid down her body to cup her bottom and haul her hard against him, and he tore his mouth from hers. "God," he groaned. "You're killing me, sweet thing."

Sweet thing. The endearment echoed in the heated dusk of the evening. Mike had called her that exact same name!

Mike. Her husband.

The thought was a bucket of ice on the flames of

her passion. She stiffened in Gray's arms, her hands sliding down to grip his muscled biceps and thrust him away from her.

He didn't protest, didn't try to restrain her, and ridiculously, that annoyed her. She didn't want him to protest—did she?—but it would have been nice to know it bothered him to let her go.

"Catherine, I—I'm sorry." Gray spun away from her. He was panting, his shoulders heaving. All she could see was his broad back, head bent as his hands fisted at his sides and she wondered if he wanted to grab her again as badly as she wanted to press herself against him and damn any consequences. "I didn't mean for that to happen."

For some reason, that was funny and she couldn't prevent a slightly hysterical bubble of laughter from escaping. "If that was accidental, what would it be like on purpose?"

He spun to face her and abruptly she stopped laughing. Even in the dark she could see the glitter in his eyes. "I didn't—I wasn't going to touch you."

There was such an odd note of agony in his voice that she almost reached for him, and she crossed her arms tightly, tucking her hands into the bend of each elbow to prevent herself from making an even bigger mistake. "It's all right," she said lamely, knowing even as she said it that it was inadequate. Then she heard her own words. What was *she* doing comforting *him?*

"No." His tone was definite. "It's not." He stepped back and her hands dropped uselessly to her sides. He was so obviously unhappy with himself; and probably with her as well, that the last small fires of desire that had burned in her system despite her withdrawal, wavered and died. Shame was beginning to curl at the edges of her consciousness and she covered her face as she turned and fled.

When the wall of the house stopped her retreat, she reached for the handle of the screen door, head down, wishing she could just drop through the ground and be done with it. "I'm sorry. I didn't intend for this to happen, either." Her voice sounded like a stranger's. "We'll...stay out of each other's way. It will be all right."

But it wouldn't be all right, he thought an hour later, lying in the middle of the big bed in the Thorne cottage guest house. His body burned at the mere memory of her soft flesh cradling him; he so desperately ached for release that he had to clench his fists to keep from reaching down and temporarily taking the edge off the raging need he felt.

He didn't *want* a temporary fix. What he wanted, in a perfect world, was Catherine Thorne in his bed, beneath him, her limbs curling around him as she took him into her willing body. What he wanted was to see her smile as if her world was complete when he walked into the room. What he wanted was the right to open his arms and have her little boy toddle into them.

Hell. When had he started allowing himself to think that those things were possible? It would never hap-

pen. *Could* never happen. Catherine could barely
stand to talk about the person who had received her
husband's heart, much less meet the fellow. She
would be beyond furious if she ever found out that
the man with whom she'd just shared the steamiest
kiss this side of heaven was a transplantee *with Mike's
heart.*

Dammit! He hadn't meant to put his hands on her,
never should have given in to the urge to rub the
tension from her narrow shoulders, to feather his
thumb across the vulnerable flesh at the base of her
neck.

But he had. And when she'd responded so instantly, so completely, he'd lost what little objectivity
he'd had around her.

And now she was ashamed of herself.

That was the thing he felt worst about.

And that, he decided the following morning, was
something he had to rectify right away. Not later today or this evening, not in a few days, but immediately. He didn't want Catherine blaming herself for
what had happened between them in the rose garden.

So after his solitary breakfast of cereal and a banana, he trudged over to the big house and knocked
on the kitchen door. As he'd hoped, she and the little
boy were already up. It looked as if they were just
finishing their own breakfast, and he said a quick
prayer that Patsy wouldn't come in while he said what
he'd come to say.

Just then, Catherine's eyes met his through the
glass panes in the door. The heat that sizzled between

them gave him such a rush he was surprised the glass didn't melt.

But if she'd felt it, too, she hid it well. She dropped her gaze from his without a single change of expression to indicate that she'd even seen him. But since she changed course and started for the door, he knew she had.

"Good morning." She had opened the door but stood in the tiny space as if afraid a few molecules of air might sneak by her and go free.

"Catherine." He nodded. Hesitated. "Could I talk to you for a moment?"

It was her turn to hesitate. She glanced back over her shoulder at Michael, who was busy slopping cereal all over his tray while he watched a popular children's music program on the television built into the cabinets. "Just for a moment." She clearly wasn't thrilled about it but he knew she was too well bred to refuse outright without a good reason.

She slipped outside and pulled the door shut, keeping her hands behind her back on the knob. The position pulled her shoulders back and thrust her breasts against the thin cotton of her soft knit shirt, and he could no more keep his gaze from assessing the tender curves than he could stop breathing.

As he watched, mesmerized, her nipples drew into taut little buds that pushed against the shirt.

She hastily let go of the knob and moved her hands and he forced himself to meet her eyes. Her face was pink.

"Look," he said, "last night was not your fault. It

was mine. I don't want you beating yourself up over it, okay?"

She didn't move. Didn't give any indication that she'd even heard him.

"I came on to you, remember? You didn't do anything wrong."

She laughed then, but there was no amusement in the sound, only an ugly self-mockery that was echoed in the bitter eyes she raised to his. "You weren't exactly forcing yourself on me, Gray. You barely touched me and I climbed all over you like—like some stupid vine, remember?"

Oh, yeah. He remembered. She'd wound herself around him as if she wanted to absorb him into her skin and he'd nearly given in to the raging need to pull her to the ground and bury himself within her. But he said none of that.

He let her words hang in the air between them for a moment. Then he said softly, still holding her gaze, "I remember all too well. I spent most of last night remembering." He sighed. "Catherine, you're a beautiful woman. And I'm attracted to you like I've never been attracted to a woman before. But—" He couldn't stop himself from raising his hand and running the tip of his index finger down over the peach-soft skin of her cheek. "I know you're still in love with your husband, no matter what your body says."

Shock filled her eyes, swiftly followed by tears.

"I'm sorry," he said again. Leaning forward, he pressed a gentle kiss to her forehead, then forced himself to turn and walk away. He wanted to take her in his arms and comfort her. He wanted to feel her mouth under his again, to share the passion that burned inside her, to know that she knew who she was kissing. But he could never touch her again. He'd already gone far beyond the boundaries he'd promised himself he'd stay behind for the few short weeks he would be in her life.

Then a new and disturbing thought rose: He might leave her life very soon, but she would be in his forever.

She got her first paycheck the following week. It came in a plain white envelope handed to her by her office assistant, with an amused, "Don't spend it all in one place."

Catherine smiled in return, but beneath her cheery expression, she was mentally calculating exactly how far her meager paycheck would go. With the savings she would net from doing the landscaping herself, keeping only Aline to help with the household chores, downsizing the BMW she'd driven until last month and not opening the swimming pool this year, she would be very close to breaking even. Thankfully, there was no mortgage on the house, but she had to be careful about setting aside some for taxes.

It struck her, as she climbed into the midsize American-made sedan she'd purchased after she'd gotten rid of the Beemer, that she almost *enjoyed* the challenge the family budget had presented. The only thing was, she qualified, it would be so much easier if Patsy didn't continue to cling to the misguided belief that money and the Thorne name were synonymous.

She sighed. It was hard to fault Patsy for not wanting to face the truth. The woman had lived through so many tragedies in her life that Catherine imagined she simply couldn't face one more.

Her mother-in-law had lost three babies prematurely before she'd finally carried Mike to term. Patsy's paintings from those years had grown steadily darker and more disturbing; Mike claimed his father had worried that she would try to take her own life.

But after Mike had been born, she'd found purpose and meaning again. Even when her beloved husband had died far too young, she'd had Mike to keep her going. And when Mike had been killed…Catherine wondered, not for the first time, how different their lives might be today if she hadn't been pregnant.

Twenty minutes later she pulled into the driveway of her home and drove around to the large garage, empty now except for Patsy's Lexus, Mike's restored Boxster that she desperately hoped to save for Michael, and the space where she parked her own humble little car. Gray parked in the single-car garage attached to the guest house.

Gray.

She hadn't let herself think about him yet today. But she hadn't been able to prevent thoughts of him from invading her mind in the five days since that night in the garden.

Oh, God, that night…the merest memory of it made her chest tighten and her hands shake as she reached for the doorknob. Had she ever known such—such *heat* before?

She'd been wrestling with a shameful feeling of disloyalty from the moment she awoke in the mornings until she fell asleep at night. And even then, she dreamed of Gray. Vivid, erotic dreams of things she'd never done with Mike, unbelievably intimate things that made her blush all over just recalling those dreams.

She'd been perfectly sane and normal until Gray MacInnes had waltzed into her life. She'd never had feelings like these, dreams like these. She'd never caught herself daydreaming of what it would be like to make love with a man, never wondered how his hands and his mouth would feel on her skin, never wondered what he looked like beneath the trappings of clothing.

Maybe it was her age. Weren't women supposed to reach sexual maturity later than men? God, if this was what sexual maturity felt like, it was no wonder teenage boys were such dopes. She felt like her whole life could be governed by one specific aching part of her body if she didn't fight the feeling.

Somehow, though, it was comforting to think it might simply be a physical process beyond her control. It wasn't Gray. It was just her age. Gray was the only man in her life, however peripherally. Gray was the only man who'd kissed her since Mike had died. It was no wonder that her errant sexual yearnings had focused on him.

But…

Mike had never made her thighs feel loose and her panties wet with a mere glance. He'd always taken care to arouse her when they made love, and he'd learned what she liked and what turned her on most, but...she'd never experienced such a deep-seated physical longing for a certain man's body.

When Gray's eyes had dropped to the front of her shirt, she'd had an insane vision of herself tearing the shirt off over her head and drawing his head down, pressing his hot mouth against her needy, aching breasts.

Was it Gray and only Gray? She'd sat across a desk from the president of a local business today while she'd been presenting a fund-raising proposal, and she hadn't felt the slightest urge to jump the man.

Not the way she wanted to jump Gray.

Abruptly closing the door behind her, she leaned back heavily against the cool wood, pressing her palms to her burning cheeks. What was she thinking?

In two short weeks, Gray MacInnes had turned her into someone she barely knew! In fact, it almost seemed that he knew her far better than such a short acquaintance warranted, no matter how physically intimate that one incident had been.

"I know you're still in love with your husband, no matter what your body says."

The words had been delivered in a gentle, understanding tone that belied the heat in his eyes. She had been too stunned by the words to respond as he'd walked away. Not stunned to consider that she still loved her deceased husband—but shocked to realize that she couldn't even bring Mike's features clearly to mind anymore. Shocked, and so distressed that she couldn't prevent the tears that had sprung to her eyes.

When had that happened? When was the last time she'd really tried to recall his face? It was a sobering realization. Yes, Gray was right. She did still love Mike…but in the way that a woman loves the memory of a life past. It occurred to her that somewhere in the bustle of surviving life's daily grind, she'd accepted widowhood. Accepted that Mike was gone and would never be back.

And as Gray's face swam before her again, she realized that for the first time, she'd even accepted the possibility that someday there might be another relationship, perhaps even another marriage, in her future.

Oh, not with Gray MacInnes. He might trip her switches with a million different circuit overloads, but she couldn't risk getting involved with him. Even having him staying on the grounds was enough to start the more vicious of the gossips talking.

No, Gray wasn't on her dance card. Not now, not ever, but someday, perhaps…someday, she would find someone who made her feel as…as alive as he did.

Of course she would.

Five

It was nearly suppertime the following evening when Catherine came downstairs, Michael on one hip. Patsy had invited Gray to join them again and he'd accepted on the condition that they not make a special effort for him. She was taking him literally. He might change his mind about special efforts after he'd been subjected to a meal with her son, who thought forks were drumsticks to use on his tray.

She headed for the kitchen to see how Aline was doing with the meal, and left Michael there with her when he wanted to sample the biscuit batter. As she walked to the drawing room to see if the wet bar was stocked, Patsy came into the room with a sprightly walk. "Oh, I'm so glad it's almost summertime!"

"So am I." Catherine smiled at her mother-in-law's good spirits. "I love seeing all the flowers come to life again."

"And our vacation is just around the corner. Just think of how much fun the beach will be for Michael this year. I can hardly wait!" Patsy straightened a doily beneath the porcelain statue of an angel.

"Patsy…" Catherine swallowed. She'd been dreading this conversation, trying to think of how best to approach it for days. But since the opportunity had presented itself, she might as well get it over with. "We won't be going to the beach until the third week of September this year. I've rented out the house during our usual time over the Fourth of July."

"You've…?" Patsy stared at her as if she couldn't possibly have heard correctly. "But we *always* go over the Fourth, dear. Since Mike was a baby, we've reserved the first two weeks of the month for ourselves."

"I know." Catherine crossed the room to sit on the footstool before Patsy's chair, putting her hands over Patsy's. A surge of tenderness rushed through her at the feel of the gnarled joints. "But you know I'm concerned about watching our pennies. I thought if we rented it out during the high season and took our own vacation in the off-season, it might pay for itself and we wouldn't have to sell it. And I have to consider my job now, too. I can't take two weeks off so I only blocked us in for one."

She held her breath and looked fixedly at their joined hands, waiting for a storm of protest. But there was only silence. Finally, she dared to glance at her mother-in-law's face—and was stunned to see tears streaming down the wrinkled cheeks.

"Patsy!" she cried.

"I'm sorry," Patsy said, her voice choked with sobs. "I haven't meant to be thoughtless about money, dear. But I did so treasure those times at the beach, and I was so looking forward to seeing Michael on the sand in a few weeks. September seems ages away," she finished forlornly.

"It's just a few extra weeks of anticipation," Catherine said stoutly, as much for her own benefit as for Patsy's. It hadn't been an easy decision; she had no desire to become the one who shattered Thorne family tradition.

"Yes." Patsy slowly eased herself to the edge of the chair and rose. "Yes, I'm sure you're right." She began to move toward the door to the hall.

"Where are you going?" Catherine asked. "Dinner will be served in just a few moments, and Gray should be here anytime." She'd even been counting on Gray to provide a distraction after Patsy had absorbed the initial shock.

"I can't eat," Patsy said softly, and Catherine could see her shoulders shake. "Please give Gray my apologies; I'm going to rest for a while."

Catherine's heart sank. Surely Patsy was kidding. "But—you love it when Gray comes to dinner. You don't want to miss that, do you?" She heard the cajoling tone in her own voice, but Patsy didn't stop.

"I'll see you in the morning, dear."

There was a dead silence in the room as Catherine

stood, listening to her mother-in-law's footsteps recede as she mounted the stairs. The lump in her throat grew to the size of a small boulder, and though she swallowed repeatedly, she couldn't control the sweep of emotion; tears began to flow as she took several hitching breaths of pain.

She took several steps and sank down on the love seat, her head in her hands. It wasn't fair. It just wasn't fair, she thought as anger rose, hot and choking. Mike had never let on that they were having financial difficulties, so when he'd died, it had been a terrible shock to learn that the family investments had taken a serious hit and that they'd been living almost hand-to-mouth for the past few years.

They could have cut back if they'd known, she thought resentfully. All those years of driving expensive cars, keeping unnecessary household help, lavish gifts and equally lavish entertaining, vacations several times a year…why hadn't he simply told her they had to live a little more frugally?

Then she thought of Patsy's shattered expression of a few moments before. All right, it would have been terribly hard on him to have to explain their monetary woes to his mother. But it wasn't any less difficult for her. Especially now, alone, without any support. A rare moment of abject self-pity swept through her. She couldn't afford the luxury of giving in to her own sorrows very often, but right at the moment, she—the moment!

Abruptly, she remembered what time it was. Gray would be arriving for dinner any minute. Panicked, she leaped up and raced for the powder room. It would never do to let him see that she'd been crying.

Just as she crossed the foyer, the doorbell rang. Cuss! Hastily, she swiped her fingers beneath her eyes, hoping she'd caught any mascara smudges.

She could hear Aline coming from the back of the house, and Michael's quick little baby steps pattering along as she walked to the heavy front door and pulled it open. "Good evening, Gray. Please come in."

As always when their eyes met, that hot, intense sensation flashed through her and she had to work not to let it show.

"Good evening." His voice was deep and quiet, and he smiled slowly at her, melting the few brain cells that hadn't been sizzled by the initial eye contact. But the smile faded almost instantly as his gaze roamed her face, and consternation wrinkled his brow. "Have you been crying?"

"Of course not." She smoothed a hand self-consciously down the side of the simple lavender skirt she'd paired with an ivory camp shirt and fought the urge to stammer. "Allergies."

He didn't call her a liar aloud, but the single raised eyebrow and the doubtful look told her she hadn't fooled him one bit. Then his eyes softened. "I don't like to see you unhappy."

Had his tone really been that intimate, that concerned, or had she given it a personal inflection that hadn't existed? Hastily she changed the subject. "I guess Patsy told you we took you at your word about dining informally.''

Gray wore khaki trousers that clung to his strong thighs, and a lightweight white knit shirt with the collar open. In one big hand he cradled a metal cookie tin, which he handed to her. ''She did,'' he said, ''and I brought an informal dessert.''

Curious, she pried open the tin. As a wave of delicious baking scent drifted out, she inhaled deeply. ''Ohhh,'' she sighed. ''Butterscotch brownies. Butterscotch is my all-time favorite flavor.'' Then she remembered the last small gift he brought. ''You either have an informant or the best luck in the world,'' she said, laughing. ''First my favorite flower, now my favorite cookie.''

Gray's smile wavered and faded as a strange look entered his eyes. They looked almost haunted. Was it worry? Guilt? *Ridiculous,* she thought to herself. *Don't be ridiculous. What could he possibly have to feel guilty about?*

''Coo-kie!'' Behind her, Michael and Aline had entered the hallway.

''Hello, Gray,'' Aline said. ''Hope you like roast beef.''

''Love it,'' Gray answered, ''especially if it's as good as those tarts you gave me the other day.''

The housekeeper smiled. ''It will be,'' she promised. Then she turned and headed back the way she had come. ''I've got biscuits in the oven,'' she announced.

''Mama!'' Michael acted as if he hadn't seen her

in several years. He made a beeline for her legs, almost knocking her off balance as his sturdy little body slammed against her knees.

Gray cupped her elbow and steadied her, and she was acutely aware of his nearness and the heat of his strong fingers searing the bare skin of her arm.

"Coo-kie, coo-kie, coo-kie!" chanted her son.

"After dinner," she said, looking down into his wide blue eyes.

His eyebrows drew together and she recognized the signs of impending storm clouds. "Now," he demanded.

But Catherine shook her head. "After you eat your dinner."

Michael stared at her for a moment, clearly gauging her resolve and his chances of success. Then she could almost see him give a mental shrug as he changed tack. "Eat *now*," he said.

Gray laughed. "You don't miss a trick, do you, buddy?"

Michael looked up at their guest. "Mac eat now, too." It wasn't a request.

Gray looked at Catherine. "Are you ready to eat?"

She shrugged. "I suppose so. Patsy won't be joining us tonight. She's not feeling well. So unless you want a drink, we can go right in."

"I'm fine." He shook his head. "Is Patsy going to be all right?"

Catherine nodded. "She should be fine by tomorrow." She handed him the tin again, then bent and picked up her son. "Come on, sweetie, let's go wash our hands."

"Mac wash." Michael twisted around to peer at Gray over her shoulder. "Coo-kie?" he asked hopefully.

Gray laughed. "After dinner," he reminded Michael. Beneath his breath, she heard him say, "Although you get points for persistence."

Dinner wasn't the ordeal she had feared without Patsy's presence, thanks to her child. They ate in the kitchen, as Gray had specifically requested when Patsy had invited him again, and Michael played favorites with Gray throughout the meal, offering him food and letting Gray feed him while refusing his mother's advances with peas and carrots.

Gray asked question after question about the little boy, and she was warmed by his interest and the way he handled Michael. He would make a wonderful father one day.

That thought inevitably led her to a more personal speculation—what would he be like as a lover? His hands, so gentle with her son, were enormous. They looked more as if they were fashioned for construction work than for designing buildings on paper. Would those hands be gentle on her body? Her breath came faster as she imagined him drawing her closer, opening the buttons of her blouse with surprising dexterity and sliding one warm, rough palm inside, cupping her breast and teasing her with his long fingers.

"Catherine?"

She jumped, and as her gaze flew to his, a flush of

heat warmed her cheeks. Gray was looking at her with a curious half smile, his eyebrows lifted. "Penny for your thoughts," he offered.

"Not a chance." She knew her voice was too fervent, and another wave of heat surged through her. Oh, God, how embarrassing to be caught in a prurient daydream by the object of her thoughts.

"All right." He grinned at her.

She kept the conversation light throughout the rest of the meal, focusing on Michael. She'd probably bored Gray silly with talk of her son, but he was the single most important thing in her life, so Gray would have to deal with that if he wanted to—wanted to what?

She was driving herself crazy with this stupid speculation!

Michael had finished his cookie at last, and she rose, thankful for the diversion. As she lifted him from his high chair, she said, "Okay, buddy, time for a bath."

"Bath!" Michael trotted off down the hall as fast as his little legs would move.

She smiled at Gray. "He loves to splash." Abruptly, she became aware of her breach of etiquette. "Oh, dear. I'm terribly sorry I don't have time to offer you an after-dinner drink or coffee—"

"Don't touch either one." Gray dismissed her concern with one offhand gesture.

"Oh." She glanced back at the hallway down which her son had disappeared, wondering what he might be getting into. "Well. Then. I'm sorry to toss you out on your ear but it's important to keep him on a regular schedule.''

''Could I—that is, would you mind if I came along and watched?'' She was surprised by the request and even more surprised when he flushed a deep ruddy hue. ''I've never been around kids much,'' he said, spreading his hands sheepishly, ''and believe it or not, I'm fascinated.''

''I believe it,'' she said lightly. ''And I don't mind at all.'' *Liar.* ''Follow me.''

As she walked down the hall and up the back stairs to where Michael's bedroom and bathroom were located just a short distance from her own, she was very aware of Gray's large body following closely behind her. The bathroom seemed too small and intimate with him looming at her side. To cover the nerves that danced inside her, she said, ''I am constantly amazed at how quickly his mind is developing. In fact—'' she shot him an innocent smile ''—I'd be happy to let you bathe him and I'll watch.''

His eyebrows rose. ''Hmm, is there an ulterior motive in that offer?''

She laughed. ''You bet. I could stay dry!''

Gray laughed, too. ''Thanks, but I'd better just watch this time.''

The kid was a wild man in the bathtub. He had his mother soaked within five minutes, and Gray escaped only by standing well out of range of the little hands that sent merry plumes of water winging every which way.

Catherine still wore the skirt and blouse she'd worn at dinner, and Gray wondered if she would have changed into old clothes if it hadn't been for him. He had to give her credit—she didn't seem to mind Michael's splashing and loud squeals of merriment. In fact, she joined in, picking up a little rubber fish, filling it with water and squirting it all over his belly. Each time she stopped, the kid would shout, ''More!''

When the bath ended and she had wrapped the wriggling child in a large bath sheet, Gray began to excuse himself. ''I'll wait downstairs while you get him to sleep,'' he said.

''Mac, 'tory!'' Michael said in a definite tone, peering out from beneath the towel with a grin as his mother carried him into his bedroom.

''What did he say?'' Gray asked. Tory? Surely the kid was too young for history lessons.

''Story,'' Catherine clarified as she wrestled the little boy into a pair of disposable absorbent underpants and pajamas. ''He loves books, and it sounds like you've been elected to read the story tonight.''

He was taken aback. ''Me?''

''You.'' She chuckled. ''Don't look so horrified. His favorite book is about a dog named Spot, and he's got it memorized. All you have to do is turn the pages and read a little. He'll supply anything you forget.''

''All right,'' he said slowly. ''Where do I sit?''

She pointed to a large rocker in the corner. ''He'll sit in your lap.''

Okay. He could do this. Maybe. He lowered himself into the rocker, then reached up automatically when Catherine swung the little guy into his arms. As she handed them a big white book with splashes of bold colors and a funny-looking hound on the front, Michael squealed and let loose a string of chatter that Gray didn't begin to understand. He looked helplessly at Catherine for a translation.

She was moving around the room picking up toys and turning back the sheet in the crib. As she straightened, he saw that the entire front of her shirt was soaked from the bath.

And transparent.

Beneath the lightweight shirt, she was wearing a white bra that must have been pretty lightweight as well, because through both layers, shirt and bra, he could see the distinct dark shadow of her nipples. The fabric clung to every curve, every taut peak, outlining her breasts as faithfully as if she wore nothing.

The gentlemanly thing to do would be to look elsewhere and pretend he hadn't noticed. Yeah, like that was possible. He couldn't tear his gaze away, watching as if in a trance while she bent and picked up the towel and her breasts bobbed and swayed gently with every motion.

She glanced over at them then, catching him in midstare. Her face changed the moment their eyes met and she froze like a doe at the side of the road. A warm red tide of color rose from her neck to her hairline, but she didn't look away. Her lips parted slightly, soundlessly, and in her eyes he saw the same erotic awareness that he was feeling. Desire, need, pure lust and yet something more…

Michael squealed again, squirming around in Gray's lap to babble another incomprehensible phrase at him. Gray winced as the baby bounced enthusiastically, pinching an all-too-sensitive piece of his equipment and he quickly shifted the child.

He cleared his throat. "What's he saying?" His voice came out hoarse and raspy, a stranger's low growl.

"He's telling you he loves Spot." Belatedly, she raised the towel and hugged it to her chest.

He couldn't help smiling. "Too late," he said softly.

She didn't pretend to misunderstand, and her blush deepened.

"You're beautiful," he told her over the baby's head. Michael was turning pages with gusto, oblivious to the adults in the room.

"I—thank you," she said in a strangled tone. Then, as the child slammed the book shut, she addressed her son. "Time to go night-night, Michael." She stepped forward, holding out her arms. "Tell Mac goodnight."

With a vigorous shake of his blond head, the little boy twisted around again in Gray's lap, scrambling up to clutch Gray around the neck in a stranglehold.

Reflexively, he put his arms up to hold the child, and his heart contracted at the feel of the small, chubby arms, the freshly bathed baby shampoo smell, the sound of the little guy's breathing, ragged in his ear. He closed his eyes tightly, all sensual thoughts erased in the sweetness of the moment. Turning his head slightly, he pressed a kiss to the shining crown of the baby's head. "You are really something, pal," he murmured.

Standing carefully with the child still in his arms, he looked over Michael's head at Catherine. "What now?"

"Now we put him down for the night." She indicated the little crib in the corner. Her eyes were soft and as he approached she dropped a kiss on the baby's head. "Night, sweetie." To Gray, she said, "Lay him on his back and give him that blanket with the silky edge."

He did as instructed, hanging over the crib to watch the kid snatch up the blanket and rub it against his cheek. As he did so, the little eyes began to close almost at once.

Gray glanced at Catherine, eyebrows raised.

Her face was alight with a tender smile, laughter in her eyes, and she put a finger to her lips as she beckoned him out of the room and closed the door quietly behind them. "He loves to brush the silky edge of the blanket over his cheek. It never fails to put him right to sleep."

He was surprised at how easy it had been. "I thought you had to rock babies to sleep."

She shrugged. "I did when he was tiny, but he's just developed that habit and I encourage it. His doctor says it's important for him to be able to fall asleep on his own." She looked away from him in the darkened hallway. "Would you like a drink—oh, I forgot you don't drink."

"I don't need a drink," he said quietly, "but I'd enjoy spending a little more time with you." *Kissing you. Touching you.* But he didn't say that aloud. She'd already retreated behind those walls of reserve she usually kept so high, and he sensed that she didn't want to talk about what had happened in the nursery.

She hesitated for so long he thought she was going to refuse. Finally, she said, "I'd like that, too," in a faint voice, as if she wasn't really sure. "Let me change my shirt and I'll be right down."

He couldn't resist. "You don't have to change on my account."

"I'm not," she said in a more sure tone. "I'm changing on *my* account. I can't engage in conversation with a man whose eyes are glued to my chest."

He lifted a hand and let the tips of his fingers caress the satiny skin of her cheek and jaw. "We don't have to talk."

Her gaze searched his in the darkness as she lifted a hand and covered his, not pulling it away, just holding on to his fingers there in the semidarkness of the landing. "I need to get to know you better," she said quietly.

He nodded. "All right." Then, before he could do something he would surely regret, he turned and headed down the stairs to wait for her. *Before what?* he wondered. There had been a promise implicit in that statement but he was afraid to consider what it might have been. He was in too deep, he knew, over his head in waters he'd never expected to enter. But that was before he'd seen Catherine, before he'd held her in his arms on a dance floor and she'd felt like she was a part of him that he'd been missing all his life.

She joined him moments later, attired in a sensible knit shirt that wasn't too clingy and certainly wasn't wet. "Thank you for helping with Michael," she said as she entered the drawing room where he waited.

"Thank you for allowing me to help," he said. "He's an amazing little guy."

She smiled with maternal pride. "I think so. It was good for him to have someone other than Aline, Patsy and me involved in his bedtime routine."

"You've never had a baby-sitter?"

"Other than Aline or Patsy, no. And you're the first man he's ever spent any time around at all."

The words satisfied him deeply, in some primitive way he couldn't define. But all he said was, "He handled it pretty well."

She nodded. The she walked to the bar and bent down to the small refrigerator beneath the counter. "Would you like fruit juice? Or a soda? I also have bottled water."

"Water would be great, thanks." He accepted the glass with ice and the bottle that she handed him and took a seat on the sofa.

Catherine curled up at the other end, arranging pillows behind her back and kicking off her shoes and tucking her bare feet beneath her. "So how's the house coming along?"

He smiled, angling himself to face her. "Fine. I'll be out of your hair soon."

"That's not why I asked!" She sounded horrified that he would think she was that gauche. "Are you pleased with the design?"

He nodded. "Very. Once it's finished I'll give you and Patsy a tour."

"I know you said you don't want to use your solar window design in everything you do. Have you included them in this?"

He shook his head. "No. Actually, I'm installing something new, an experimental window that I just developed. That way, if it's a flop, I won't have inflicted it on anyone but myself."

She smiled. "But then you'll be stuck with it."

He shrugged. "I'll renovate."

She was studying him with eyes that he felt saw far more than normal. "You're uncomfortable when you talk about designing with your windows. Why?"

He smiled wryly. "I just don't want to be known as 'the solar window guy.' I'd like to design stunning things, no matter what materials I use, and be recognized for the quality of my designs."

"And that's been tough since the windows became such a hit," she surmised.

He nodded. "That about sums it up."

She was nodding as if she understood, and he felt an odd sense of gratification. "Why did you decide to expand your firm?"

He shrugged, wishing she'd curled up in the circle of his arm instead of clear at the far end of the couch. "I was in an accident and I had a lot of time to think while I was recovering. Design has always been my first love. I have some very creative, competent people in the Philadelphia office and I knew I could manage them from a distance, so I decided to try the Baltimore market."

She was looking at him curiously, clearly distracted from talk of architecture, and his mental defenses went on high alert. "What kind of accident?"

"A freak one," he said dryly, deliberately keeping his tone light. "Unlikely to happen to anyone again in a million years, they say. I used to play rugby, and I got kicked in the torso. Wound up with severe internal injuries."

She looked horrified. "I never thought of rugby as a particularly rough sport."

"I bet you never thought about it much at all," he teased.

She smiled. "No, I suppose I didn't. It's similar to soccer, isn't it?"

"Somewhat, but a lot less civilized. Maybe someday when it's rained for a week and you're bored silly I'll explain the difference." He grinned.

She smiled back. "So what kind of injuries did you have?"

Damn. He'd been hoping he wouldn't have to lie outright. "Ah, a number of things were wrong," he said, making a vague motion somewhere in the region of his stomach. Well, that was true enough. "I had surgery and then post-op recovery took a while. That gave me time to research several cities to see where my best chance at expansion lay."

"And Baltimore was the best choice."

He nodded, relieved that she seemed to have been diverted from his injuries but again unwilling to lie outright. What would she do if he said, *After I found out my donor heart came from Baltimore it was the only choice?* "There were three top contenders on the Eastern seaboard. Baltimore is close to Philly, the climate is pleasant and when I visited, I liked the area."

She smiled, picking up her glass for a sip. "The climate's not always so pleasant in the dead of winter."

"I don't mind a little cold weather," he said. "But Boston, for instance, is a little farther north than I really want to be. And Orlando in the summer? Forget it."

"Those were the other two choices?" she asked, laughing. "From one extreme to the other."

"Exactly."

There was a small silence between them, a warm, comfortable moment that he wished would never end. Then he remembered how she'd looked when he had arrived. She'd clearly been crying; there were red marks around her eyes and the tip of her nose had been shiny and pink. "Catherine?"

"Yes?"

"Why were you crying earlier? And don't give me that line about allergies again."

She sighed. "It's a long story—"

"Is Patsy seriously ill?" It was the first thing he'd thought of, even though she had reassured him earlier, and the most dreaded.

"Oh, no." She was genuinely shocked. "There's nothing like that wrong with her."

"So why the tears?"

She heaved another sigh. "I postponed our family vacation. We always go over the Fourth, but this year, with my new position, it works out better if I wait until early September to take time off. Even if it is part-time," she said defensively, "I can't just drop everything and leave whenever I please."

"Did Patsy expect that?"

"No. Not at all. She was just…disappointed. She said she had a headache and she decided not to have dinner with us. I felt badly for upsetting her."

"Ah." He nodded. "You two seem to have a nice relationship. I thought wives were supposed to loathe their mothers-in-law."

She laughed, and warmth shot through him. "Not in this house. I couldn't be luckier. She's terrific."

There was another silence, but it wasn't quite as comfortable as the first. Finally, he said, "I'd better be going." When she didn't demur, but nodded assent and rose, he was disappointed. After the moments they'd shared upstairs, she was back to acting as if they were mere acquaintances.

He let her walk him to the door before he turned and spoke again. "I enjoyed tonight. I enjoyed it a lot." He lifted his hands and lightly ran his palms up and down her upper arms in a gentle caress. "Tell me you did, too."

Her eyes searched his face before she ducked her head and said, "I did, too."

"I'd like to spend time with you and Michael again."

Her head came up. "Why?"

He let the amusement show. "Because I'm wildly attracted to you and I think your kid is fantastic?"

"Good answer. But before I agree, you need to know that I'm not looking for any kind of…involvement."

"How about fun and friendship?" She might not want to admit it, but they were already involved. He hadn't intended to do more than observe her when he'd first come to the city. But now he saw how futile it was to try to stay away from her.

She was smiling hesitantly. "I suppose we could try that."

"So what would you like to do?"

He waited as she thought. "We could have a picnic. Michael loves being outdoors."

"When?"

"Tomorrow? It's Saturday, so I don't work."

"Sounds good. I'll come by at noon."

When she nodded, he dropped his head and brushed one quick kiss over her lips. He wanted a real kiss, wanted to feel her wrapped around him, pressed against him, responding as she had that first time out in the garden, but he sensed she was struggling with herself. And though he didn't know why, he wasn't about to give her any excuse to back out. "See you tomorrow," he said, and left.

Six

She should have her head examined. She should have said no. Well, no thank you, actually. She couldn't get involved with Gray MacInnes. Shouldn't. Wouldn't.

Catherine set the bagged sandwiches in the cooler and opened the refrigerator, reaching into the hydrator for oranges and apples. Michael loved oranges if she cut them into small pieces so he didn't choke on the stringy fibers. She began peeling the oranges, her mind automatically turning back to thoughts of Gray.

He was rolling in money. She was scrambling around trying not to lose her son's family home. Gray would think she was after his money. Everyone would. And that was possibly the one thing that horrified her the most.

When she'd married Mike, she knew what was said behind her back. *She's after his money. She knew which side her bread was buttered on. I wonder what she had to do to get him to marry her—why else would he have married someone so unsuitable?* The last was from the disgruntled mama of one of society's belles of the upper crust.

She had ignored it then, because she'd genuinely loved Mike and they'd been so happy that the insults had largely rolled off her back. And Patsy had loved her from the beginning as well. Patsy had deflected the sly words with amusing stories about the persons in question, and her acceptance of Catherine had smoothed the path. Catherine's own deportment and good taste had done the rest.

But she didn't ever want to be subjected to that again. Despite Mike and Patsy's insulating effect, the hateful attitudes had cut deeply into a young girl's sensitive soul.

And now…now it wasn't just her. Now there was Michael to consider.

She put the oranges and apple slices in a container together; the oranges would keep the apples from turning brown in the air. What else? Banana chips, another of Michael's favorites. A few of the gingersnaps Aline had made yesterday, lengths of cut celery, and drinks.

Anything she did would reflect on her son, she thought as she added napkins and zipped the insulated picnic bag closed, and she was determined that he grow up feeling at ease and fully a part of his father's world. A wild fling with a wealthy bachelor was *not* part of the plan.

And it would be wild, she thought with a little shiver as she recalled the hot blue fire in his eyes last night. He'd looked at her as if he'd like to lie down with her right there on the floor. If Michael hadn't been there, who knew what would have happened?

But Michael *had* been there. Thank God. She felt her lips curve up as she thought of how the big, dark-haired man and the tiny boy with the nearly white hair had looked, nestled into the rocking chair where she'd once nursed Michael.

They had looked so right, so perfect together, that it was impossible not to entertain the obvious thought: they had looked like father and son. Despite the difference in their coloring, there had been an intimate tenderness in the moment that had melted her heart. Gray might not know much about children, but if he didn't like Michael, he was an Oscar-caliber actor.

"Here she is," Patsy sang out as she entered the kitchen with Michael, whom she had dressed in a bright red shirt and a little denim romper with trains chugging across the front of it. "Look, Mama's got your picnic all ready to go!"

"Thank you for dressing him," Catherine said to her mother-in-law. "Are you sure you don't want to come along?"

Patsy smiled. She seemed to have gotten past the unhappiness of the night before and was her usual cheerful self. "Since when have you known me to enjoy a picnic? Ants, flies, sitting on the ground…"

She gave a mock shudder. "No, thank you. Anyway, I have a decorating committee meeting for the Iris Affair at one."

The Iris Affair was a benefit dinner-dance for the local women's shelter. It was held every year in June, and all the ladies on the committee traditionally grew dozens of delicate irises in glowing jewel hues which were used on the night of the event.

Catherine sighed. "I'm nervous since it's just going to be the three of us."

"That's not a bad thing," Patsy said gently. "You're allowed to have a date, dear."

"It's not a date," Catherine said firmly. "It's just a—a get-together. I'm not even sure how he talked me into it."

Patsy only smiled. "He's a very good-looking man. Maybe you should turn it into one."

"I'm not interested in dating. I've got you and Michael. Why do I need someone else?"

Patsy's lively face sobered. "You won't have me forever, dear. And Michael's going to grow up and lead his own life before you know what hit you. You're still a young woman with a lot of years ahead of you."

Ooo-kay. There didn't seem to be a good answer to that. "It's just a casual thing," she finally said, working at convincing herself as much as she was at convincing Patsy. "I was going to take Michael out for a picnic lunch, anyway."

Patsy just smiled again. "You have a good time." As if on cue the doorbell rang. "I'll get it," she said.

Catherine took a deep breath, checking the diaper bag she planned on taking in case—well, in case. Moments later, Patsy came back down the hallway with Gray behind her.

"...haven't had horses in the stable for more than a year now. Catherine sold Mike's gelding a few months after the accident. She said it was just too difficult to look at poor Spruce out there with no one to ride him."

Not to mention the fact that it cost a small fortune to feed and care for him, Catherine thought, wondering how on earth they had gotten on to that topic so quickly. The last thing she wanted was for Patsy to blab more of their personal concerns to Gray. "Hello." She forced herself to meet Gray's eyes with a friendly but impersonal smile. "Are you ready for this picnic?"

"Ready to rock and roll," he said. "I'll drive. Did you have a place in mind?"

She raised her eyebrows. "Oh, I wasn't thinking of leaving the grounds. We have some lovely spots right here."

"All right." He looked a bit surprised for a moment but recovered quickly, picking up the picnic carrier. "Lead the way. I'll be the pack mule."

She couldn't help smiling. "Now there's an image I can't quite wrap my mind around."

"Bye-bye." Patsy waved at her grandson as Catherine picked up Michael and the three of them trooped out the back door. "Have a lovely time. Don't forget the sunscreen."

"Already put some on both of us," Catherine assured her.

"And his hat."

"I have that, too. You know, if you'd come with us, you could make sure he doesn't get sunburned."

Patsy's smile became a wicked grin. "Good try, dear. I'll be the one lounging in the air-conditioning when you get back."

"She doesn't like picnics?" Gray asked as he ambled beside Catherine across the lawn. After putting his little cap on his head, she set down Michael so he could walk. Gray, too, wore a hat. He'd pulled a billed cap from his back pocket when they'd gotten outside, and tilted it down so that most of his face was shaded. Beneath the brim, his eyes were a brilliant blue.

"Patsy's not much of an outdoor person. She loves flowers, but only if someone else plants and weeds them, and her idea of camping is a night at a budget motel."

He laughed. "Silver spoon syndrome, huh?"

"Um-hmm. Patsy came from a wealthy family and when she married Mike's dad, she came into an inheritance from her grandmother. That was separate from the Thorne fortune, of course."

"But of course," he said, smiling wryly.

"I suppose that's why she's a bit unrealistic about money," she said, sighing as she watched Michael charge ahead of them. "She just doesn't seem to grasp the concept of budgeting."

"So the family finances have fallen to you since your husband passed away."

She shot him a startled look. "Yes. By default, although I don't usually mind."

"How did you get to be so knowledgeable about money matters? You hold a degree in English literature."

"How did you know that?" She stopped dead in the path. She was almost certain—no, she was dead sure she hadn't told him that.

He stopped, too, and a look she couldn't interpret flitted across his lean features before he shrugged and smiled. "I don't recall. Patsy probably told me. How else would I know?"

"I don't know." Slowly she began to walk again but her mood had changed. She didn't know why, but she felt a strong sense of uneasiness. Not fear, just a sixth sense that warned her something wasn't quite right.

"Catherine?" Gray snapped his fingers in front of her face. "You in there?"

"Yes. Sorry." She couldn't imagine what was bothering her, and she made an effort to shake off the feeling. "Why don't we spread the blanket over here? There's a nice patch of shade beneath that tree." She wasn't eager to discuss her finances with Gray, and it *was* a pretty spot. Although she did all the landscape work now, she still had a local youth come in and mow the grass. He'd just been there the day before, leaving a clipped carpet of lush green.

It was a warm June day and the little clearing was

hidden from the house by a copse of trees interspersed with blooming mountain laurel in shades of pink and white. Michael chased around a big ball Gray threw for him, and moments after he showed the little boy how to kick, Michael landed an amazingly lucky shot that scooted several yards across the yard. Gray chased it, and she watched as he came back across the grass kicking the ball with his feet and doing several sly tricks, such as keeping the ball in the air by bouncing it on his knees. It was obvious that he was well coordinated and that he'd spent many hours practicing maneuvers like that one.

She stretched out on her side, watching the two. Gray was patient and encouraging, and he handled Michael's short attention span with aplomb. When Michael kicked and connected with the ball, Gray's head whipped around toward her. "Did you see that? He's a natural athlete."

He didn't wait for an answer but turned his attention back to her son. Catherine watched him thoughtfully. There had been a distinct ring of pride in his voice. Almost as if…as if Michael's ball-playing skill was a personal point of pride. But why would that be? He'd only met her son a handful of times, and really barely knew either of them. *So why, then, do you feel that you already know him, that you can talk to him like you haven't talked to anyone since Mike died?*

A few minutes later, the ball game ceased to hold Michael's interest and he was entertaining himself by turning and turning in big circles on the grass until he fell, giggling and too dizzy to stand. But as soon as he could stand without losing his balance, he would begin to spin again.

Gray dropped down beside her on the blanket and she quickly sat up. Reclining felt just a little too intimate and vulnerable.

"He's terrific," he said. He took off his cap and tossed it on to the blanket, running his fingers carelessly through his dark hair. "In a few years he's going to be a mainstay of a soccer team."

"I worry about what's going to happen as he grows older," she confessed. "I can't teach him all the boy stuff he's going to need to know. I went to all-girls' schools my whole life!"

Gray laughed, but his eyes were understanding. "I don't think you have to worry. Michael may not have a father figure in his life, but he'll have plenty of male role models if you get him involved in sports and other activities. On the other hand, he *does* have what's most important—a stable, loving home."

"That's comforting. I hope you're right." But she knew it would still worry her. Then she remembered he spoke from experience. "I guess you do know what you're talking about," she conceded, "since you grew up in a similar manner and you've turned out just fine."

Gray's eyebrows rose. He turned his head to watch the little boy as he spoke. "There are few similarities between my childhood and Michael's, trust me." He gestured to the beautiful spot around them. "Michael's never going to have to worry about whether or not you'll be able to pay the rent or buy food for dinner.''

Not if I can help it. Then defensiveness kicked in and suddenly, it was important to her that he not think she'd grown up taking wealth for granted. ''Before...you asked me how I learned to handle money.'' She pleated the blanket between her fingers. ''I didn't grow up wealthy, either.''

Understandably, he looked a little surprised. ''You didn't?'' His smile was crooked. ''You've adapted well.''

''As have you.'' She inclined her head briefly. ''My father was a librarian at the University of Maryland. We weren't going to get rich on his salary, but we should have been able to live comfortably. We didn't.'' Her voice was flat. ''I learned early to check the mail and hand-carry the bills to my father, then watch while he paid them. It was the only way to keep our utilities from getting turned off.'' She shook her head. ''I learned when he got paid and made him give me grocery and rent money. Sometimes he would surprise me and come home with what he told me was a bonus. He'd tell me to spend it on clothes, but I saved as much as I could for the weeks when he didn't bring home enough.'' *Or any.*

Understanding began to dawn in Gray's eyes. ''What was he into?''

''Gambling,'' she said. ''After his death I found all kinds of betting stubs in his office. I wasn't even sure what they were until Mike told me.''

''That must have been tough to handle.'' He put

out a casual hand and rubbed it up and down her back in a comforting gesture. Unfortunately, her senses were finely tuned where he was concerned, and her body reacted to his nearness and his touch, her heart racing and her breathing growing shallow in anticipation.

Annoyed at her inability to control her reactions to him, she moved restlessly, dislodging his hand and leaning back on her elbows. "It was. I worshipped my father. It was terribly hard to see him in a whole new light. My father, addicted to gambling the same way some people are addicted to drugs or cigarettes."

She lapsed into silence, contemplating the past. Gray didn't speak, didn't move to touch her again, maybe sensing that she needed a few moments. They watched Michael turning and turning on the grass while birds chirped and the peace of the day soothed raw wounds she hadn't let herself think of in several years.

Finally, he stirred. "Why did you just tell me all that?"

She was startled. "I—I don't really know. I guess…I guess it's important to me that you understand who I am, that I'm not just some spoiled little rich girl." The words were out before she really thought about what she was saying.

Gray turned toward her. "It's important to me to understand you." He raised a hand and cupped the side of her face, tilting her chin up with his thumb as he leaned toward her. "Just for the record," he murmured, "I never would have characterized you as 'a spoiled little rich girl.'"

She closed her eyes as his face drew nearer and then his mouth was on hers, warm and firm, shaping and testing and teasing until she began to kiss him back, letting him pull her up against him and clasping his shoulders. He parted her lips and his tongue slipped inside in search of hers, playing a gentle game of seek and retreat. Fire began to kindle low in her belly and she moaned beneath his mouth, sanity threatening to flee. "Michael," she finally managed.

Gray lifted his head abruptly, tearing his mouth from hers as his chest heaved. "Sorry."

Her head drooped like a flower too heavy for its stem, and her forehead fell against him as she took deep draughts of his clean, male scent. "You weren't going to touch me, remember?" She spoke breathlessly, her face buried in his neck.

He cleared his throat, and his voice was sober, an odd note of self-recrimination clear. "I remember. But I can't seem to stay away." He drew back far enough to look into her eyes. "I think about you all the time."

She swallowed. His honesty deserved the same in return. "I think about you, too." She smiled, though the effort was painful. "I'm not ready for this...but that doesn't seem to matter when you touch me."

His eyes darkened. "If we were alone," he said in a deep, low growl, "I'd be tempted to abuse that knowledge." His hand lifted. "I'd touch you here—" His fingers drifted along her cheekbone and stroked down her neck with a featherlight touch out along her collarbone. "—and here." The tips of his fingers whisked quickly over one already-taut nipple and she sucked in a sharp gasp as a bolt of sexual pleasure shot straight down into her loins. "I'd slide my hand down here," he went on, trailing his fingers down her belly, and I'd *definitely* touch you here." One long finger slid between her legs and pressed firmly right over the throbbing flesh covered by her panties and shorts.

"Stop," she gasped, grabbing his thick wrist and dragging his hand away.

He smiled down into her eyes. "And then—" He turned his arm and grasped her hand in his own, drawing it to his lap. "—it would be your turn to touch me." He held her palm over the full column of his arousal, and she gasped again as his flesh leaped in response. Her fingers automatically curved to cradle him, and his jaw clenched as a sound of pure male need escaped him. He dragged her hand away from his body and pressed a kiss to her palm before linking their fingers. "But I won't, because you're not ready for that."

She wasn't sure her voice would work and she cleared her throat before she tried it. "Actually, I think I am." She tipped her face up to his, meeting his heated gaze full-on. "You said before that I was still in love with my husband, and you were right. Part of me will always love Mike, but he's a memory now. It's time to move on." *Way to go, Catherine. So much for not wanting to get involved.*

Gray drew in a harsh breath. He tore his gaze from hers and looked blindly up at the sky. "You know," he said in a conversational tone, "your timing really sucks."

She laughed, breaking the sensual spell that bound her; she suspected he'd said that on purpose. "Yours isn't much better."

His smile carved a deep dimple in his cheek. "Wanna bet?"

Michael came running toward them then, bored with his solo game, and she began to set out the food, grateful for the chance to recover her balance after Gray's last provocative comment.

Afterward, her son's little head began to droop, and they headed back to the house so Catherine could put Michael down for a nap. Gray insisted on carrying the child, leaving Catherine with the empty—and hence, much lighter—basket.

As she moved with them back across the lawn and up the steps to the kitchen door, she was riveted by the sight of the sleeping child cradled in Gray's arms, his small head resting against Gray's heart.

Although it wasn't her nature not to plan, she decided that she was not going to think too much about where all this was going. There were simply too many variables, too many obstacles, for her to predict, or even allow herself to dream about the future.

But…how could there *not* be a future with Gray in it? A few weeks ago she hadn't imagined she could love again. Now, she was afraid she was dangerously close to doing exactly that.

* * *

Catherine invited him to an evening barbecue, another picnic and two more family dinners in the following week. In the evenings, Patsy took Michael off for his bath after dinner, giving them moments of privacy that Gray looked forward to the way a prisoner longed for the day of release.

He knew what he was doing was wrong. He'd lied to her—sort of—and now he'd waited far too long to tell her the truth. She would hate him if she ever found out.

It couldn't last. He was the first man who'd touched her since her husband died. One day she would realize he was just an ordinary guy, and she'd move on. One day this would end, and he would get out of her life. But until the day that she grew tired of him, he didn't have the strength to leave.

Right now, all he could think of was Catherine. When he wasn't with her, he thought about her. Of the way her hair fell straight and shining down her back on the rare occasions when she didn't twist it up, of the way the muscles in her long, slim legs flexed as she stooped to pick up her child, of the way her sweet little bottom filled out her shorts, of the way she lowered her head slightly when she smiled into his eyes.

Of the tender way she kissed her son's temple when he laid his head on her shoulder, of the gleam of laughter in her eyes when she gently teased, of her determination to keep the only life her mother-in-law

had ever known running smoothly despite the agonizing loss they'd suffered.

Of the way her mouth moved under his, the way
her soft body felt in his arms. Of how desperately he
wanted to take her down to the floor and bare her
silky flesh to his eyes, mouth and hands.

After Patsy had taken Michael up to bed one evening, he waited until Catherine joined him in the family room. They'd gotten into the habit of watching the
news and discussing it. And kissing. As he watched
her walk toward him, he thought about how ridiculous
it was that the highlight of his day was a single quar-
ter hour in the evening when Catherine sank down
beside him in the circle of his arm. How lucky he was
to have this chance at all.

God, he'd nearly blown it with the stupid comment
about her degree the day of the first picnic. He still
didn't know why he'd blurted that out. But as he had,
he'd had a vivid, undeniably accurate mental image…*she wore a graduation cap and gown, and she
ran full-tilt toward him with a smile as she waved her
diploma. He held out his arms and she ran right into
them, alternately laughing and crying between kisses.*

*"The only thing that could have made this day bet-
ter is if Daddy had been able to be here."*

"I know." He blotted her tears with his thumb and
kissed her again. *"I wish he was here, too. But you
know I will always take care of you, don't you?"*

Thinking about it gave him an unsettled feeling.
He'd begun to remember more things, and in more
detail, than could possibly be explained rationally.

Most of the time he simply refused to think about it. But occasionally, his unique perception reared its head and he couldn't avoid it.

Like when he'd been kicking the ball with Michael in the yard. The thrill that had shot through him when the kid proved adept at it was pretty intense. *Too* intense, maybe? As if the part of Mike Thorne that lived within him had been proud of the little guy's prowess. As if the guy was still determined to be a part of his family's life in the only way he could.

And then Catherine sat down, curling up in his arms as if she'd done it forever, and thoughts of her scattered everything else churning in his brain.

"Hi," he murmured, turning his head to nuzzle a kiss beneath her ear. "Everything under control during bath time?"

"Everything's fine." She tilted her head slightly, giving him better access to the sweet taste of her there, just along her jaw, and her voice was breathy.

He lifted a hand and turned her face toward him, seeking her lips, satisfaction coursing through him as she sank against him with a quiet murmur of pleasure. He drew her across his lap, cradling her in one arm as he bent his head and kissed her deeply, repeatedly, until she was turning her head blindly seeking his mouth, until they both were dragging in harsh gasps of air as if they'd run side-by-side marathons.

He stroked her hip and cupped her breast through the light summer blouse she wore, feeling the nipple rise even through her bra. He'd made himself a promise that he wasn't going to put his hands beneath her clothes, or shove them up out of his way, or, best of all, remove them entirely, in her home. He didn't quite know why, but it felt important to him and so he doggedly stuck to it night after night even though sometimes he could barely think enough to remember the vow. He was so heavily aroused he ached, and her hip squirming and pressing against him was the sweetest torment he could imagine. But—he silently gritted his teeth—he wasn't going to take any chances on Patsy walking in on something that had gotten out of hand. And once he touched Catherine the way he longed to, the way he dreamed of in fevered nights of tossing and turning, he knew there would be no stopping.

And so, with one last deep kiss, he began to gentle the intensity of the contact, stroking her arm and shoulder rather than her breast, shifting her from the helplessly abandoned pose across his lap. "We must be crazy, torturing ourselves like this."

"Possibly. Probably." She was still in his lap, the smooth coil of her hair mussed and her lips red and slick from his kisses.

"I never thought that at the ripe old age of thirty-two, I'd be trying to make time with my girlfriend in the living room, listening with one ear for her mother to walk in."

Catherine laughed. "Number one, she's not my mother. Number two, you're not *trying* to make time. You're succeeding." Then she cocked her head. "Is that what I am? Your girlfriend? Somehow, I have a difficult time envisioning myself as both a mother and a *girlfriend.* Mothers don't date."

"Deal with it," he said, dropping a kiss on the top of her straight little nose. "And speaking of dates, would you like to go out to dinner and/or a movie Friday night?"

To his surprise, she hesitated. "You could come over here for dinner," she offered instead.

He studied her face, instinct raising alarms inside him. Something was wrong. She'd withdrawn slightly, although he couldn't imagine what he'd said that might have caused such a reaction.

Carefully, he said, "I've joined you for dinner a number of times. I thought it might be nice to dress up a little and go out."

"I'd much prefer a quiet evening in," she said. "I'm feeling a little stressed between the job, the volunteer work and the family commitments. I need time to get used to the change. Would you mind?"

He did mind, but this didn't seem like quite the time for a frank answer. He could tell from the way her body had tensed and she'd closed up that she would refuse him altogether if he tried to push her. "No," he said, "I don't mind, but why don't you let me cook for you for a change? I've been meaning to have a meal on that pretty little terrace behind the guest house, anyway."

She smiled and her body relaxed immediately. "That would be lovely," she said. "May I bring something?"

He shook his head, bemused by the way the tension

within her had dissipated. He mentally reviewed the conversation again, still trying to figure out what had happened. ''Just yourself.'' At least they would be alone. And as he realized just how alone they would be, his body forgot that it was supposed to be cooling off. Dammit. He'd really hoped to walk out of here before Patsy came back down. Now it looked like he'd better sit right where he was for a while longer.

Seven

Patsy still hadn't come back down half an hour later. When Catherine went to check, fearing that Michael was being difficult about getting to sleep, she returned to report that her mother-in-law had developed a headache and had gone on to bed.

"All right." Gray stood, crossing the room to where Catherine stood in the doorway. "I'm going to head home. Walk me out."

He put an arm around her waist as they walked through the house to the back door, but when he turned to face her, she said, "I'll walk part way with you."

The night air was warm, redolent with the scents of summer: fresh-cut grass, honeysuckle, and the pretty yellow climber roses. It was nearly nine, and dusk was finally falling, the bright colors of Catherine's gardens dimming. Overhead, a sliver of moon was rising and a few ambitious stars were battling the last scant rays of light.

He took her hand and they went down the steps. "It's a beautiful night."

"Um-hmm." She sounded relaxed, happy. Clearly she'd forgotten the tense moments after he'd asked her to go out on Friday evening.

Her small fingers were threaded through his, and he wondered if she ever thought about how distant and cautious she'd been when they first met. He did, and was still amazed that he could be here, strolling with the woman who had haunted his dreams, touching her and talking with her nearly every day.

They strolled in silence for a moment. Then, "Look," he said. "Fireflies. I used to catch dozens of the poor little guys in one night. I'd have so many that my jar would be permanently lit up when I brought them to show my mother."

"I always wanted to keep one as a pet," she said. "And my father would help me make a cozy little house in a jar, with grass and a bottle cap full of water…but when I'd come down in the morning and check, the firefly had always escaped. My father would shake his head and say, 'Doggone it. I must have made those holes too big,' even if they were tiny little pinpricks in the lid. I fell for it for years before I realized he was letting them go, but by then I didn't care."

He realized he was smiling as he swung their

joined hands slightly. ''Maybe later in the summer when it gets dark earlier, Michael can stay up long enough to see them. We could help him catch a few and put them in a jar. Wouldn't he love that?''

She hesitated so long that he thought she wasn't going to answer him, and he felt an immediate sense of dread surround him. ''Catherine? What's wrong?''

''Nothing.'' But her voice sounded uncertain.

He stopped, drawing her to a halt in the middle of the path. ''What's going on?''

She sighed. Was silent. Sighed again. ''Is there going to be a 'later in the summer'?''

The question took him aback. It was the first indication he'd had that she was thinking long-term. As aphrodisiacs went, it was one of the most powerful he'd ever known. His heart gave a leap that literally left him breathless.

He took her by the shoulders and smiled down at her, not caring if she saw the love for her that he could no longer deny in his eyes. ''If you want one, there will be,'' he assured her.

Unable to wait, he cupped her shoulders in his hands and lowered his mouth to hers in a sweet pledge. After a scant moment, her mouth softened beneath his, and her hands fluttered up to clasp his wrists. Her mouth opened and her tongue danced out to meet his, and when he slid his hands down her back and cupped her bottom, she made a sweet little needy sound and her leg twined around his thigh as it had the very first time he'd ever kissed her. Here, in this same garden, although they were a good deal farther away from the house than they had been then.

Annoyance faded, replaced by a rising awareness of how alone they were, standing here in the quiet of the garden. And as that thought registered in his hazed brain, he suddenly acknowledged what his subconscious had been thinking since she'd walked out the door with him: he wanted her. Tonight. Now.

Anticipation instantly raced through him in an almost painful rush, arousing him far more quickly than the steady rising of his sex he'd been enjoying. He yanked her hips hard up against him and ground himself against her, drinking in the little whimpers she made as his urgency registered. They writhed and twisted for a moment, then frustration with the clothing between them guided him.

He let her slide down from his body, bringing his hands up to flick open the five buttons that held her blouse together. He dragged it off in one smooth motion, then reached behind her and twisted the clasp on her bra until it gave as well.

"Gray!" Her voice sounded panicked. "We're outside."

He stifled an urge to chuckle, then drew her a few steps into the deep shade beneath a dogwood tree along the path. She looked up at him for a moment, and *he* nearly panicked when he thought she was going to object, but then she shrugged her shoulders free of the straps and the bra fell away. He felt his heartbeat double. Her breasts weren't large but they were perfectly shaped, round and full with generous nipples crowning the tips. In the darkness, he couldn't discern whether they were copper or rose but in his mind's eye he already knew. They were a sweet soft pink, and the nipples now were larger than they'd been before her pregnancy. When he realized what he'd just been thinking, he shunted it aside, unwilling to deal with the complications of his damned memory for the moment.

"God," he said hoarsely, reverently. "You are so beautiful." He cupped the weight of each breast in his palms, slowly circling the nipples with his thumbs in the way he knew she liked—*No! Don't think about how you know that*—until the crests were rigid points stabbing into his palms and she was arching her back, begging wordlessly for more. Only then did he bend his head and suckle one sweet peak, making deep sounds of pleasure at the taste and texture of her satiny flesh in his mouth. He swirled his tongue around the nipple over and over again, drawing lightly on her until she tore herself away from him with a muffled groan.

"You," she said, "too."

Her hands moved to the buttons of his shirt, fumbling open the garment until it hung loose around his upper body. Her palms were warm, smooth and he reveled in the sensation of her fingers combing through the hair on his chest—his chest! Alarm bells clamored. If she touched his chest she wouldn't be able to miss feeling his scar. And he had no intention of letting this moment get tangled up in questions.

Hastily, he reached up and circled her wrists, tugging her hands up until they slid around his neck and into his hair, holding her there so that she hung on her tiptoes, flush against every inch of his aching flesh. Her bare breasts were hot and almost hard as they pressed against his chest; he growled low in his throat as he rocked her against him, kissing her deeply, wild with the feel of her flesh against his.

He *knew* he should tell her who he was, how he'd found her, knew it wasn't fair of him to deceive her like this, but the words wouldn't come. She was his world, the reason he drew breath, the reason he woke in the morning. He'd wanted her since he'd woken up with her face in his head, and he had to have her, just this once.

Only once, he promised himself. Or maybe twice, he amended hastily, thinking of their Friday evening date. He wanted to make his own memories, dammit! Instead of the vague snippets of whatever memory he carried from Mike Thorne, he wanted to know for himself how she felt beneath him, wanted to hear for himself the tiny sounds of fulfillment he could make her utter. He wanted to look into her eyes as he entered her, to know that she was seeing *him*.

Because he loved her. Because in a normal world she'd be a normal widow and he'd be a regular guy and they could spend the rest of their forever together. Because he could never have forever, but he was damned if he was going to forfeit his one chance at happiness without some memories to sustain him.

He unbuckled the belt she wore and opened her shorts, skimming his hand inside, deliberately teasing himself, inserting a single finger beneath the edge of the satiny panties he discovered. He dragged it back and forth across her belly, inching a little lower each time. But finally, he couldn't stand to wait anymore and he tugged the shorts and panties down in one quick motion, then lifted her free of them.

Her white flesh glowed in the darkness that had fallen, and he reverently ran his hands all over her: shoulders, down to her fingertips, back to her breasts, and down over her torso to the softness of her belly. He continued his path around her rib cage to her silken shoulder blades and down to where the sweet cleft of her bottom beckoned him to gently skim a finger beneath her, until she gave a startled cry and moved restlessly. Then he knelt and ran his hands down the backs of her thighs to her ankles and back up, settling them on her hips. Exerting a slight pressure, he urged her to close the small space between them.

"Gray," she said in a shaking voice.

"Hush," he said. "Just for a moment." He rested his face against her soft thicket of downy curls, then blew a warm stream of air against her and she gave a small cry as her hips rolled once. When he pressed against her inner thighs, she widened her stance for him.

God, he wasn't sure he was going to be able to take this as slowly as he wanted. Down on his knees, with his own thighs spread wide, he was rigid and pulsing, and the soft night air brushing over and under him was an excitingly different sensation. He shuddered, feeling a ripple of ecstasy dance down his spine, and he clamped down hard on the shreds of his self-control.

Slowly, he teased her curls apart with his tongue, finding the moist nubbin beneath and flicking his tongue over it. He refused to let himself think of anything but her, anything but the way her hips moved against him, pushing his face against her as her little sounds of pleasure increased in pitch and tempo. It was a delightful task, and finally he knew she was as ready for the next step as he was.

Sliding back from her, he rose and pulled her to him again.

"Don't stop," she gasped.

"I'm not going to." He ran his hands all over her, unable to get enough of her baby-soft skin. "Pregnancy didn't change your shape," he muttered.

"No," she said in a husky voice. "I was slender before and I only gained sixteen pounds. It was gone within two months."

Then he realized what he'd said. And as quickly, he realized that she'd assumed it was a question. Thank God.

He smoothed a hand over her belly and down to the fleecy triangle of hair that covered her mound, combing his fingers through the silky curls. "It's time to lie down," he told her.

Together, they sank to their knees. He stretched her out on the soft grass beneath the sheltering dogwood and lowered himself directly on to her, pressing her hips down and apart with his until his aching shaft was in position for the inevitable conclusion.

Catherine was quiet, and he felt a return of a fragment of the earlier tension invade her limbs.

With a sudden flash of intuition, he knew what she was thinking: in this respect, he was *very* different from her husband. "Relax," he said hoarsely. "Just relax, sweet thing." He kept talking, soothing her with his voice as he felt the tense muscles in her inner thighs relax. He forced himself to go slowly as he fit himself to her, to move just a little further each time into the slick, heated channel, to withdraw and begin again. She was wet and extremely tight around him, and he felt himself trembling with the effort to hold himself in check, to make it good for her.

Finally, he was home, lodged deep inside her, so close to the edge that he was afraid her next motion might be the end of him.

"You okay, sweet thing?" he asked her.

"I will be," she said in a quivering voice. And before he realized what she was doing, she dug her heels into the ground, thrusting her pelvis hard against him with a rolling motion that ground him directly against her sensitive mound—and she exploded. Her body grabbed like a fist around him, released and grabbed again, and then his own control was gone, and he began to plunge wildly into her, pumping his hips relentlessly as she screamed and sobbed his name, her back arching and body shuddering beneath his. Release swept through him, pushing him deep, deep within her, the jetting of his seed a moment of inexpressible ecstasy in an encounter that defined lovemaking in a whole new way for him.

When the spasms finally subsided, he realized he was gripping her buttocks, probably hard enough to leave marks. Then again, he was probably going to have marks of his own from the feel of her heels on his backside.

Her arms fell away from his shoulders and her thighs dropped wide. Her hair was a shining white sheet across the ground and he wondered fleetingly if he'd torn out her careful coil or if it had simply come undone. He raised himself on his forearms and looked down at her. "You are the most beautiful woman in the world," he pronounced, brushing a kiss across her lips.

She chuckled, a mere breath of sound. "Spoken like a man in the throes of gratitude."

He was amused by her teasing. "You bet. Eternal gratitude." He hesitated, then couldn't resist. "And did I earn yours?"

She smiled slowly, her teeth a flash in the night as she stretched languidly beneath him, and his breath caught as her body shifted around him. "You were wonderful."

The words could have been trite but her tone was so sincere he couldn't doubt her. Kissing her one more time, he said, "Much as I'd like to stay right here, I'm guessing you'd like to get off the ground."

"You guess correctly."

He raised himself away from her and extended a hand to pull her to her feet. As he did so, she staggered slightly, wincing. "Oh, hell. Did I hurt you?" He didn't care if she heard panic in his voice.

"No." Her own tone was full of humor. "Relax. I'm just not used to—I never had—" She stopped, and he couldn't help laughing at her chagrin.

"Okay. Thank you." He walked around, gathering clothing, and tossed his own garments on before helping her to dress. "I guess I'll walk *you* home now," he said.

"You might have to drag me. I'm not sure I can walk."

He knew she was teasing but he didn't care. He swept her into his arms despite her protests and carried her the whole way back to her door. Then, after he'd kissed her one more time and she vanished inside, he walked back to his own quarters.

At least, he was pretty sure he walked. He could have floated or flown, for all he knew.

The instant she opened her eyes in the morning, she knew what had occurred last night. A dreamy sigh escaped her even as she winced when muscles she'd forgotten she had protested her vigorous activity. She relived every moment that she could remember, her body tingling as she recalled his masterful touch. Good heavens. If every time with Gray was like that time, she wasn't sure she'd survive it.

Then she realized what she was thinking. Every time? True, he'd indicated that he intended to continue to be in her life, but how practical was that going to be after he'd moved into his own home?

So far, she'd managed to avoid going out with him anywhere, managed to avoid the gossip and inevitable nasty comments that would accompany any sighting of her in the presence of a man as wealthy as Gray. But once he'd moved, it would be impossible.

Okay. So she would have to be honest. She'd have to explain that she had to think of her reputation for her son's sake, if not for her own.

Over cereal and coffee after a quick shower, she practiced her speech. *The sex was great but I can't get involved with you.*

Okay, the sex was incredible but I still can't get involved with you.

I have to think of Michael, of how he'll be affected by any gossip about me.

She brushed her teeth, then checked her watch. Only eight. Michael typically slept until close to nine, and she heard Patsy stirring around in her room. Her mother-in-law would hear him if he awoke before Catherine returned.

So if she went over to his cottage right now, she could get it over with instead of worrying all day about how to nip this insane attraction in the bud.

On the short walk over, she had to stop and take a deep breath beneath the dogwood tree where they'd lain last night. There was no indication that they'd been there except for a slight crushing of the grass that no one else would ever notice.

But she noticed. And she remembered. She swallowed hard. She was a mother. A pillar of the community. She had a job now that could suffer if her reputation was sullied. She couldn't be involved with Gray.

Buoyed by the thoughts, she walked the rest of the short distance. Knocking briskly on the door, she tensed when she heard his footfalls approach.

He swung the door open. "Good morning." There was pleasure and mild surprise in his expression as he ushered her inside. Then he turned, and his face had changed from inquiring to intent, his eyes from pleasant friendliness to blazing sexual heat. Without another word, he pushed her back against the door and covered her mouth with his. His tongue thrust into her mouth in a blatant imitation of his actions last night, and she could feel the hard strength of his thighs already pressing boldly against her. A few layers of clothing were all that lay between them, and she probably would have sold her soul to be able to lift her legs around his waist and join with him again in the wild and wonderful world they'd created together.

When he lifted his mouth abruptly, she was still lost in sensual preoccupation.

"I believe I already said good morning, but now it's gone from good to great." He smiled down at her, holding her less tightly.

"Ah, good morning." She tried to gather her scattered thoughts. "We have to talk."

"No, we don't. We do pretty well without any words at all." His blue eyes sparkled, drawing her into an intimate wordless sharing. She was halfway to putting her arms up around his neck and leaning into him when she realized what she was doing, and she hastily crossed them instead.

Shaken, she looked away, and a less than comfortable silence fell between them.

''Was it something I said?'' His voice was whimsical but she sensed an underlying intensity, an unnamed tension that throbbed in the air between them.

She swallowed, shook her head.

''Then why do I have the feeling we've just taken a giant step backward?''

She sighed. ''Because we have. I have—I have to.'' She suited action to her words then, stepping a full foot away from him. ''I can't engage in an extramarital affair,'' she said baldly.

''Since you're not married anymore, I'm not sure that's accurate.'' His voice was even and easy. ''So forget an affair. How about some strictly physical, mind-blowing recreational sex?''

Her gaze flew to meet his again, and the humor she saw there made her smile. ''You're not taking me seriously,'' she accused.

''Yes, I am.'' His expression was deadpan. ''If sex is all you're willing to give me, I'll try my hardest to settle for that.''

Now she laughed aloud, the awkwardness of the earlier moment forgotten. ''I can't get physical with you again,'' she said firmly. ''It complicates things too much.''

''Some things are meant to be complicated.'' His voice was quiet and sure, and she had the impression he was thinking of more than their mutual attraction.

Before she could move farther away, he stepped close to her again and gathered her against him, lowering his head and setting his lips on hers.

Dear God. She had always thought of herself as a woman with willpower, but as his hands moved over her back and down to clasp her hips, urging her up and into him, she could literally feel her self-determination draining away. It was like every other time he'd kissed her. The moment their lips met, every brain cell she had went into hibernation. Only now...now it was even worse because she knew.

Now she knew what ecstasy lay in store for her. Resisting him wasn't just difficult, it was impossible.

With a little sigh, she put her arms around his neck, letting him part her lips and explore her mouth as her body came alight with need and desire. He was big and warm and hard against her, surrounding her with his heat as he crowded her back against the wall and pressed himself snugly against her, parting her thighs with a knee and moving between her legs.

She moaned at the intimate feel of his arousal against her tender, throbbing mound, and he swallowed the sound. Oh, she shouldn't want this, shouldn't need this, shouldn't need *him* so desperately, she thought dimly. Was this why she'd really come here this morning?

God, she hated to think so, but... But when his warm hands slipped up beneath her skirt and he hooked his fingers in her panty hose and panties, she didn't resist as he peeled them down her legs and tossed them aside. He opened her blouse and shoved it back, simply lifting a breast free of the confines of her bra so that he could take her into his mouth, and when he began to suck gently, swirling his tongue around and around the sensitive peak, she felt her legs buckle.

"No, sweet thing." His breath blasted her tender earlobe. "Stay on your feet." His hands held her until she'd locked her knees; his voice was a rough murmur as he worked his hands between them and freed himself from his pants. Seconds later, she was shocked from the sensual lethargy in which she'd been floating as his heavy shaft probed between her legs, pulsing and moving as he sought her soft entrance. He took her bottom in his big hands, lifting her and tilting her hips to receive him, and moments later, he swallowed her scream as he thrust home, beginning a strong pounding rhythm that sent shock waves from her most sensitive woman's flesh racing through her entire body. She'd expected to be sore, but he'd taken such care to ready her for him last night that she wasn't nearly as tender as she'd anticipated.

Automatically, she clamped her legs around his lean hips, clinging to him as he moved steadily within her. He dropped his head and kissed her, then the rhythm changed and she felt his control flying to pieces. He threw back his head, teeth gritted, jaw locked as he held her against the door and slammed into her again and again. There was no sound in the cottage except for his harsh breathing, her breathy moans and the insistent slap of flesh meeting flesh in a slick, sweaty, primal mating ritual. She felt her own climax gathering like a fist inside her, tighter and tighter, and she began to cry out with each thrust.

"Let go," he said in a guttural tone that barely sounded like him. "I want you to come with me." He rolled his hips heavily against her, and with a sudden surge of sensation, she began to fly apart, her body arching and shaking in his arms.

Gray growled, and his big body went rigid, pressing her hard against the door as her body tightened and clung around him. She felt the repeated pumping of his release exploding deep within her, and she tightened her legs more securely around him, loving the heavy, rolling thrusts that signaled the end.

At last they both were still. Gray kept her with him as he staggered to a nearby couch and flopped down, and she gasped as the motion drove his still-hard shaft deep into her. His eyes were closed, head lying limply against the back of the sofa, but a smile crossed his face and his hands slipped lazily over her bottom, stroking the soft flesh.

"Now *this* is the right way to start the day," he proclaimed.

She smiled against his shirtfront, just realizing that they both still wore most of their clothes.

"I wish I'd been able to sleep with you last night. I wanted to hold you all night long." His words wove warm, intimate images in her mind. Then his tone changed, and she knew he was grinning. "But failing that, this is the next best thing."

"Umm-hmm." She didn't want to talk, didn't want to move.

He pulled her blouse free of her skirt and gently scratched her back, running his fingertips up and down in a manner that made her arch beneath his hands. She loved to be touched like that—how had he known?

"What made you do that?" she asked in a muffled tone. "I love having my back scratched after—afterward."

"After you make love to me," he said with deep satisfaction. Then he shrugged in answer. "I don't know, it just seemed like the thing to do at the time."

"It was," she assured him. Somewhere in her mind was a question, but she couldn't quite draw it from beneath the sweet haze of completion that enveloped them, and eventually she stopped trying.

"Catherine?" He continued lightly stroking her back. "I hate to bring up mundane matters but do you realize we haven't talked about birth control?"

She shook her head against his shoulder. "Not a problem. I'm on the Pill."

"Oh."

"My periods were irregular after Michael was born and when they hadn't settled down after a year, the doctor thought we should try this." She felt the need to explain, though he hadn't said another word.

"It doesn't bother you that I didn't wear anything?"

Slowly, she sat up, regarding him in silence. "How

many women have you done this with in the past couple of years?''

"None."

She was a little shocked. "None without protection?"

"No," he repeated, "none at all."

"Why?" She blurted it out without thinking, too surprised to hide her astonishment. "You're single, you're healthy and you can't tell me you haven't had women interested."

"Lovemaking should mean something more than just scratching a physical itch," he said quietly. "I was never much of a hound dog, but my accident made me realize that every single thing in life is important and should be precious." •

She held her breath, wondering what else he might say, but he was silent. Did that mean that she meant something to him? She couldn't pursue the thought, afraid of where it might lead her.

Okay, so she'd been stupid to think she could stay out of his arms. She'd never had an affair before, but she supposed she was involved now, whether or not it was sensible. The thing was, an affair was a short-lived relationship. And Gray was becoming more important to her by the day.

Important enough that in the space of one short morning she'd swung from thinking she was going to have to stop seeing him to admitting to herself that she had long-term dreams where he was concerned. Dreams like rings. Dreams like wedding vows and more children.

But she couldn't say any of that to Gray. True, he'd made references to the future, but he certainly hadn't said anything specific.

Was he thinking the same things she was? She supposed that the only way to find out was to wait and see.

Eight

"**S**tay a while." He lifted her off his lap with an easy strength that secretly thrilled her, then passed her a box of tissues while he righted his clothes and walked to the door.

"I can't," she said as she tugged her skirt down, feeling incredibly abandoned and wicked as the air caressed her uncovered skin beneath it. "Michael will be waking up soon."

He nodded. "All right. I'll walk you back."

"No," she said hastily. "That's all right." Patsy might be in the kitchen and if she saw them to-gether…well, she could add. Her panty hose and underwear were a tangled heap, and she eventually gave up trying to salvage the hose, settling for bare legs and panties.

Gray was studying her, his brow drawn into a frown. "Are you ashamed of this? Of us?"

She froze. "It's not that I'm ashamed, exactly, I'm just…uncomfortable. I'm not used to sneaking around. And I don't think I'm ready for Patsy to find out we're carrying on."

"'Carrying on'?" He began to chuckle. "Is that what we're doing? Catherine, Patsy isn't blind. She probably didn't come back downstairs last night on purpose."

She stared at him. "You really think so?"

He took her in his arms, smiling down at her as he caressed her back. "I'd bet on it. Patsy might be aging, but she hasn't forgotten what it's like to be in—interested in someone."

She groaned, burying her face in his shirt. "I'm so embarrassed. What must she be thinking?"

"That you're a young woman who shouldn't live the rest of her life alone. That she's glad you're happy. That you're lucky to be with a handsome, virile stud like me."

She raised her head, unable to keep from laughing, and balled her fist to jab him in the chest. "Be serious."

He caught her fist in his hand before she could land the blow. "I am serious about some things." His eyes grew dark. "I'm serious about the fact that you are the most beautiful woman I've ever known."

She smiled. "Maybe you're prejudiced."

"Maybe." He grinned back at her, blue eyes sparkling. Then he broke into the chorus from a Broadway musical that spoke to the theme of a woman's beauty.

Catherine felt shock roll through her as she heard the familiar phrases. Mike had loved that song. He'd sung it to her often. In fact, she still had the CD around somewhere, although she hadn't played it since his death.

Gray's voice faded into silence as he saw her face. "What?"

"I—Mike sang that all the time." She was too shaken to dissemble.

Gray's eyes cooled and the animation drained from his features. "Sorry," he said in a curt tone, dropping his hands from her.

"No, it just…caught me by surprise," she protested. "Frankly, a lot of the things you do and say remind me of him."

His eyebrows rose. "Are you telling me you're with me because I remind you of your husband?"

She would have sworn there was a trace of hurt in his voice, although his face was expressionless, his manner that of a man who didn't really care about the answer.

"Of course not. That's silly."

"Is it? Why is it silly to hope that the woman you're growing to care for doesn't just want you because you're familiar?" His face changed as he spoke, becoming even less approachable, and she realized he was regretting what he'd just said.

"It's silly because it's not true," she said quietly, her gaze on his face. "It's silly because the woman you're growing to care for thinks she's growing to care for you, too, and it scares her stiff.''

Finally, his eyes softened. "Does it?" He reached for her, pulling her against him and kissing her forehead before leaning back to look down into her face again. "I'm sorry if I overreacted," he said. "I feel like I'm at a disadvantage, like I have a rival I can never measure up to."

"You *don't* have a rival," she said. She took a deep breath. "Sometimes it seems that you understand me far too well for the short amount of time we've known each other. Mike...Mike loved me but he didn't ever really understand me, my hopes, my dreams. He wanted to keep me in an ivory tower, much like his mother has been her entire life. He never understood that it was important to me to be a part of the world, to make a difference." She smiled wryly. "He'd have had a fit about me working. He would have hated it."

"But you enjoy it."

"Yes. I do." It seemed so disloyal but it was true. Mike hadn't really known what lay beneath her surface. He would have been happy if she'd been a social butterfly like his mother, an occasional volunteer at nothing too dirty or rigorous, a full-time mother content with raising her children. The first two would have made her crazy. The third...while she loved being a mother, she loved the challenge her new job presented and would feel somehow less complete if she wasn't involved in something like that. Gray understood that. And he understood her in other ways, as well. He knew what she was thinking before she even spoke, it sometimes seemed.

"I've only known you a few weeks," she said, her voice quivering despite her efforts to stay calm, "and already I can imagine you being a part of my life for…a long time. Everything I learn about you only makes me like you more."

"All right, so—"

She put a hand over his mouth. "But I have to think of Michael. I can't make mistakes that could affect him, so we have to take this slowly. Do you understand?"

Behind her hand, he nodded. Then she felt his lips brushing her palm in a kiss. He reached up and removed her hand, but held it between both of his. "Thank you for your honesty." His chest rose and fell. "I have something I want to tell you, too—"

"Could we do it later?" God, she hated to put him off, when his eyes were so blue and sincere. Some sixth sense told her it was important. "I really have to get back to the house."

"Sure." His arms loosened. "I'll walk you partway back." He smiled and held up two fingers like a Boy Scout. "I promise I won't let Patsy see me."

What a coward he was, he thought as he walked toward the house three days later. He wondered if she'd realized how relieved he was when she'd asked if he could postpone telling her his important news. Still…he'd almost told her. God, he'd wanted to. But was she ready for it?

Of course she wasn't. How could anyone ever be ready for the kind of bombshell he would drop? She said she was growing to care for him; he could only pray that those growing feelings would be enough to allow her to forgive him for deceiving her, to allow her to accept that Mike was a part of him and always would be.

He avoided thinking about just how much a part of him Mike had proved to be. How could he ever tell her that? She'd think he was insane.

That, of course, depended on whether or not he ever actually got a chance to talk with her about it. He'd been waiting, wanting plenty of uninterrupted time, which appeared to be in short supply around the Thorne house.

Although he'd eaten dinner with them the night before last, Michael had been running a low-grade fever and she hadn't wanted to leave him. He could understand that. And she'd worked extra hours this week because of a fund-raiser she'd planned and needed to oversee.

Tonight he intended to ask her to have dinner with him somewhere away from the house. Preferably in the next day or so. That was the only way he could ensure they would have plenty of time to talk—and God knew they were going to need it after he told her about his heart transplant.

She opened the door to his knock, but Patsy and Michael were right behind her, so he contented himself with giving her hand a quick squeeze.

Dinner was pleasant, and afterward he got to help

with the little guy's bath time routine again. This
time, he got in on the water squirting action, and he
was the one with the soaked shirt. When he looked
over the baby's head at Catherine, he could see in her
eyes that she was remembering what had happened
between them after the first time.

He stood silently as she put Michael down, then
followed her into the hallway. God, he wanted her.
She started toward the stairs but he snagged her hand
and pulled her back, catching her to him while he held
both her hands behind her back in one of his much
larger ones. The position arched her firmly against
him and she squeaked in surprise as he brought his
mouth down hard on hers, seeking her participation
with his tongue and exploring the curve of hip and
breast with his free hand.

"I want you," he breathed against her mouth.
"Come home with me tonight. Sleep in my bed.
Wake in my arms."

"I—I can't," she said in an agonized whisper.

And he knew she couldn't. He would never expect
her to leave Michael overnight, even if Patsy was in
the house.

"I'll come over for a little while," she whispered
against his mouth.

He wanted her to. He didn't want her to. It annoyed
the hell out of him that they had to sneak around like
this.

Later, he barely remembered the rush across the
garden path to his door. He led her through his darkened cottage to the master bedroom, tearing away

both her clothes and his own without turning on a light. He was going to tell her soon about his transplant, but tonight...tonight he had to have this memory.

The bed was big and soft, moonlight casting a weak glow among the shadows. Gray realized his hands were shaking as he pulled her to the bed, then caught her against him for a deep, stirring kiss. Catherine responded completely, pressing her smooth, bare curves against him, her small hands sliding up into his hair to hold his head down to her.

Finally, he couldn't wait any longer. He rolled to his back, pulling her astride him, groaning aloud as her legs settled on either side of him, her soft, humid woman's flesh snugly covering his turgid, aching shaft. "Take me," he urged hoarsely. "Take me now, sweet thing."

Catherine responded by shifting her body to her knees. Leaning forward slightly, she brushed her breasts over his chest as she caught his mouth with her own. At the same instant, he felt himself slip into position at her heated portal, and before he could move, she dropped herself down in one short, sharp motion, thrusting him deep into the slick, clinging channel.

He nearly came off the bed at the intensity of the sensation, and he had to force himself to stillness as she began to move above him. When she nearly placed her hands on his chest he came to his senses just in time to catch them and thread his fingers through hers, letting her brace herself on his hands, her lovely features intent and alight with her own pleasure. Watching her in the shadowed room, knowing he was giving her pleasure was an amazing aphrodisiac and he felt control eluding him.

Quickly he took her by the hips, yanking her down hard and holding her in place as he began a pounding jackhammer rhythm that brought him to the edge within moments. When he felt her begin to shatter and buck above him, her inner muscles milking him in the unmistakable spasms of fulfillment, he couldn't prevent his shout of satisfaction.

Later, he held her in the curve of his arm, one of her legs laid possessively over his, her small hand enclosed in his resting on his chest. He felt giddy with pleasure but it faded as he remembered what he had to do. He was going to have to tell her soon. They weren't always going to be making love in the dark, or partly clothed.

Making love. It was so easy to admit. He loved her. Probably had loved her since the first time he'd seen her across that ballroom, possibly even since the moment Mike Thorne's heart had begun to beat in his chest.

But all that didn't matter. What did matter was what he did with the future he'd been given.

Acting on impulse, he said, "Let's go out to dinner tomorrow night." He would get a ring tomorrow, ask her to marry him. Everything else would work itself out. It had to.

Then he realized she hadn't answered him. Her body had stiffened slightly. Pulling himself up on one elbow, he tried to gauge her expression but it was too dark. "Catherine?"

"Why don't we have a quiet dinner here?" she suggested.

He was perplexed. "Why? I'd like to take you out, let someone else pamper us." He dropped his voice. "I'd like to have you all to myself for a few hours."

"I…" She hesitated, and unease blossomed within him. "I'd really rather not go anywhere. We can be alone here."

"You don't want to be seen with me in public, do you?" he asked incredulously.

"It's not that—"

"Then go to dinner with me." It was a challenge. She remained stubbornly silent.

"I don't get it," he said finally. "You claim it's not that you don't want to be seen with me, but you've made every excuse in the book not to go anywhere that we could be noticed." He tried not to let anger color his voice. "I know I'm not exactly a blue blood, but I thought you cared."

"I do care," she cried. "But people said terrible things after I married Mike and I couldn't bear it if they started again."

"What kind of terrible things?" He still didn't get it.

"I was a gold digger," she said bitterly. "I married him for his money, I snagged a rich husband, I did all kinds of immoral things to get him to marry me. If they said those things then, just imagine what a

field day they'll have when everyone finds out—''
She stopped abruptly.

"Finds out what?" This was the key, he was sure
of it.

"That we're nearly insolvent," she said heavily.

Of all the things he'd expected her to say, that
wasn't even on the list. "You're…having money
problems?"

"Mike had money problems," she said, a fierce
flare of anger in her tone. "I have no money, just the
problems he left me with."

Suddenly, he saw it all clearly. The coupons, the
job, selling Mike's horse, all the damn house and yard
work she'd been doing. "What did he do?" he asked
harshly. God, her father had been a gambler who'd
given her childhood hellish moments. He felt fury rising, hot and choking. How could Mike have done
something similar?

"It wasn't really his fault," she said defensively.
"You know how bad the economy was. I don't know
all the details—he made some bad investments. All I
know is that when he died, we had next to nothing.
Even his life insurance had lapsed."

He was too shocked to speak.

"You can't tell Patsy," she said quickly. "Please.
She doesn't really know how bad it is. I've tried to
make her understand that we have to be careful with
our spending but—"

"She hasn't made much of an effort," he said
grimly, recalling Patsy's blithe dinner invitations. At
last the horrified expression on Catherine's face made

sense. She'd probably been mentally calculating how much it would cost to feed someone his size!

"She can't help it," Catherine said, and it infuriated him that she felt she had to defend her mother-in-law. "She's never been in a position to worry about money. It's hard for her to grasp how serious the situation is."

"She's going to have to," he said firmly. "You're doing a hell of a job, but you can't do it without making her cognizant of the sacrifices she has to make as well."

"Don't you dare say anything to her," she flared, apparently guessing his intentions. "She's my family; I'll deal with her as I see best."

"Even if it runs you into the ground," he said scathingly.

Her whole body stiffened, and she pulled completely away from him, sliding out of the bed and fumbling around for her clothes. He let her fumble while he hunted up his own shirt, aware as always of the scar that cleaved his chest. Finally, shirt and pants dragged on, he reached over and snapped on a lamp beside the bed.

Catherine blinked in the light, but her motions didn't slow for an instant. "I'm going back to the house now," she said in a distant, implacable voice.

"Catherine." He reached for reason. "We have to talk about this."

"There's nothing to talk about."

"The hell there isn't." Desperation was a sour taste in the back of his throat. "You're willing to sleep with me but you won't be seen with me because someone might think badly of you? That's nuts!''

Her face froze. "It is not. I have to protect my son.''

"Your son could not care less what people might say right now," he shot at her, "and by the time he is old enough that it might matter, nobody will remember or care anymore.''

"In a few years," she said, "I might be able to get my finances to the point that I wouldn't feel like I'm taking advantage of your wealth.''

"That's what this is really about, isn't it?" He was furious. "*Your* perceptions of what people might think. The way *you* feel. My God. You'd actually consider waiting *years* to marry me because of ridiculous reasons like that?''

Her face, already porcelain in the scant light of the single lamp, drained of all color. "Marriage?" she whispered.

"What the hell did you think I was offering you?" he said, his voice a sharp blade that made her flinch when it landed. "A long-term sexual arrangement? Thanks but no thanks.'' He stepped around her and held the bedroom door open. "I'll walk you back.''

They hadn't spoken in three days. Catherine knelt in the grass by one of her shaded perennial beds, adding some colorful impatiens and other annuals to give it color now that the spring's riotous show of blooms had ended.

Michael played a few yards away from her, kicking

a bright yellow ball through the grass. He'd already looked at her beseechingly several times and asked, "Mac?"

And each time, a fresh arrow of pain struck her heart.

Gray wanted to marry her.

Every time she thought of the fight they'd had, tears welled in her eyes again. She felt as if all she'd done over the past few days was battle tears.

He wanted to marry her. At least, he had until he'd realized how stupid and hung up she was about her money problems. Which, now that she really thought about them, weren't as big a deal as she'd believed. As she had *chosen to believe,* she thought, angry at her own mulish tunnel vision.

Especially not in light of the fact that she might just have ruined her chance at happily ever after with Gray. He—

"Michael!" Gray's voice was a distant shout. "No!"

She whirled, realizing that she'd been planting with a vengeance, unaware of how much time had passed. Michael was all the way down at the bottom of the yard—standing on the apron around the sunken swimming pool. The swimming pool which she hadn't had filled this summer because it was too costly to keep open. The swimming pool which, she saw in horror, was plainly visible through the large gate that stood wide open. Had she left it open after she'd trimmed the bushes inside yesterday? She couldn't be sure but she was very afraid she might have.

She rose as Gray came from the direction of the cottage, running at full speed toward the edge of the pool. But even then it was too late. Her son took one toddling step forward and pitched over the side of the pool with a startled shriek that almost instantly cut off into a silence even more frightening than the sight of the fall.

"Micha-ae-el!" She hadn't known she could scream like that.

Gray reached the pool before she did, vaulting over the side, and she could see him as he bent. He straightened immediately. "Call 9-1-1," he ordered her.

"Is he breathing?" She stopped in her tracks, torn between the need to go to her baby and the knowledge that Gray felt he needed expert medical attention.

"Hurry!" His voice cracked like a whip and she leaped into action, racing back toward the house to place the call.

"Patsy!" she screamed as she entered the house. Her mother-in-law appeared just as the emergency dispatcher came on the line, and she saw Patsy's face crumple as the older woman realized what had happened. After relaying the initial information, she thrust the phone at Patsy as she rushed back out the door, grabbing two beach towels on the way. "They want someone to stay on the line. You can't go too far from the base or your reception will break up."

She didn't remember running back down the length of the yard, scrambling into the shallow end of the pool beside Gray—thank God he'd only fallen three feet instead of twelve!—who was kneeling with his hand on the little boy's wrist. Keeping track of his pulse, she realized as she saw him check his watch.

Michael was frighteningly still, his little body limp. Blood seeped out from beneath his head and she made an agonized sound when she saw it.

"Don't move him," Gray said sharply when she went to gather him into her arms, so she settled for covering him with the beach towels despite the warmth of the day.

After that, time passed with agonizing slowness. Michael was breathing, but showed no signs of consciousness. "Come on, little buddy, wake up," Gray said at one point, but the child didn't rouse. In what were probably mere minutes but seemed like forever, an ambulance was there, screaming right down the lawn as Patsy hurried along in its wake.

The medical technicians were calm and efficient, relaying information to a base as they immobilized her son's neck and took vital signs. They got out a backboard and gently moved Michael on to it. Gray held his head, his expression as agonized as she knew her own must be.

As she scrambled into the ambulance and it screamed out on to the road toward the hospital, she saw Aline in the driveway. Patsy was already in the car and Gray snatched the keys Aline tossed him just before he slid into the driver's seat.

The ambulance attendants were just unloading Michael when Patsy and Gray came rushing in. A nurse stepped in front of them as they all moved forward.

"Parents only," she said. "There's a waiting room right over there." She pointed to a small room.

Catherine felt Gray hesitate, and she slid a glance up at his drawn features. "I need you," she said, not caring how it sounded or what he thought.

Immediately, he slipped an arm around her and said, "Let's go."

"I'll wait," Patsy said.

They followed the nurse to the cubicle. When the nurse pushed aside the curtain and showed them in, the doctor was already stitching a wound on the back of her son's head. There was blood everywhere and Catherine put a hand over her mouth with a moan.

"I should have been watching him more closely." Her voice broke. "I was distracted and—"

"It was an accident," Gray said firmly. "That little stinker is fast. And smart. I bet he waited until you weren't looking." He paused. "He's a tough little peanut. He's going to be okay."

The words almost shattered the rigid self-control she was maintaining. "Mike used to talk all the time about having some little peanuts of our own some day," she informed him, trying to smile.

Gray's face froze for a moment and the thought chased across her mind that it bothered him when she spoke of Mike. His tone was neutral as he said, "Let's see what the doctor has to say." He led her around to where she could lean over and comfort Michael, and everything faded except concerns for her baby, who began to calm down as soon as he saw her.

"He can't feel this," the doctor explained as he quickly closed the cut. "Looks like he just split it open when he fell. He's going to have a terrific bump there, though. When we're done here, they'll be taking him upstairs to radiology for some head scans."

"Do you think he's concussed or has a skull fracture?" Gray asked.

"There are no indications so far that he suffered any further injury," the doctor assured them. "But given the distance he fell—I understand he fell several feet on to concrete?—it's precautionary."

Gray asked several more questions that she only partly registered, preoccupied as she was with comforting her son. They let her stay with him when they took him up for the scans, while Gray went back out to the waiting room to update Patsy and reassure her.

Six hours later, Michael was discharged after a short observation period revealed no additional concerns. Gray drove them home and carried the little boy inside, and she heard the emotion in his voice when he kissed her son's forehead and said, "We'll play ball in a few days, little buddy. I promise."

She followed him out into the hallway. "Thank you. He'll look forward to that."

Gray paused at the top of the steps and turned toward her. There was pain in his eyes. "I'm moving out. I'll come back and play ball with him, but I'll be out of the cottage this week. Please extend my thanks to Patsy."

"But…is your house ready?" She hadn't expected this.

"No." He shook his head. "I've gotten another condo."

"Because of me?" she asked baldly. "Gray, you don't have to go. I—"

But he had already turned and started down the stairs. "I can't do this. Can't you just let it alone?"

No, she thought. She couldn't. Not when it was her future—and his—at stake. He'd said he wanted to marry her. He couldn't just turn off the feelings that went with that, could he?

Nine

She didn't have an opportunity to get away until the following morning when Patsy said, "Have you thanked Gray yet for all his help yesterday?"

Catherine shook her head. "No. I really need to, though."

"Why don't you run over there now?" her mother-in-law suggested. She gestured to Michael, who was lying on the sofa singing along with a children's musical video. "He'll be fine and I promise I won't let him out of my sight."

"I know you won't." But still she hesitated, smiling wryly. "Rationally, I understand that he'll be fine. But my irrational side isn't reassured by that, unfortunately."

Patsy smiled. "I understand. His daddy fell out of

a tree when he was nine and knocked the stars out of his head, just like Michael. Fifteen stitches. It took a while before I let him go out alone again.''

''All right.'' Oddly, the story, which she'd never heard before, reassured her. ''I'll only be gone a little while.''

She went straight out the back door and along the path to the cottage. It was a beautiful summer day, and as she approached, she saw that Gray had the windows open in the living room. The white curtains were billowing out and lazily floating on the slight breeze.

As she passed them, she glanced in—and then stopped and looked again.

Gray lay on the couch, sound asleep. He lay on his back, bare-chested, with his shirt wadded up in one fist and clutched to his chest as if he'd grown hot and slipped it off just moments ago. His face was turned toward her and her heart turned over at the sight of his beloved features. *I love you,* she told him silently.

Then, with a jolt of clarity, she saw that she didn't have to say it silently anymore. He'd said he wanted to marry her, brushed aside her silly worries about the money issues, and he'd been right. It was their life together that was important. Who cared what anyone else said or thought?

She'd hurt him deeply, she knew. Now all she could do was try to fix it and pray that he still cared enough to forgive her.

She crossed to the door and tried the knob, pleased when it opened easily. Silently, she crept across the floor and knelt on the floor beside him. His T-shirt lay across his upper chest but she could see the ridged plates of muscle across his abdomen, and she raised a hand and leisurely drew a finger across him there, just above the top of his jeans. His stomach muscles contracted and she smiled, repeating the gesture, playing with the crisp arrow of hair that disappeared beneath his jeans.

She bent her head and placed a kiss on the forearm across his chest, then propped her chin there and waited until his brilliant blue eyes opened.

"I'm sorry," she whispered. "For the other day. For—everything."

He was silent. His gaze was steady on her face. Finally, just when she was about to begin babbling, he said, "I believe you."

That was it? The small bubble of hope she'd allowed to build inside her slowly deflated. Still…she had to try. She swallowed. "Gray, I love you. If you still want to marry me, I'll feel like the luckiest woman in the world."

Slowly, a smile began to curl at the edges of his lips. His eyes crinkled at the corners. "Oh, I still love you," he assured her. "And there's nothing I'd like better."

Her heart doubled its rhythm. She wanted to leap up and kiss him, but she restrained herself, aware that they needed to air all the issues between them. "I didn't," she said slowly, "want you to ever wonder if I married you for financial security."

"Believe me," he said, "I've never thought you

needed me for financial security. And now that I know the truth about what happened after Mike died, I'm certain you don't need me. You managed to avoid financial ruin by being very, very careful.'' He snorted. ''And I don't have any hang-ups about having a working wife.''

''Mike did. We had some terrible fights because I wanted to work.'' The memory sobered her. ''I feel disloyal for even saying it. I loved my husband. But he was very content to have me be a housewife with my days full of society events and volunteer work.'' She made a face. ''It doesn't take much to manage a house when you've got a housekeeper, a maid and a gardener. I was going *crazy* trying to fit into the mold.'' She spread her hands. ''Mike's role model was Patsy, whom he perceived as the greatest homemaker ever. I'm very different from Patsy. Not better, just different. I need challenges.''

''Perhaps his view of his mother was a bit narrow as well,'' Gray said quietly. ''Patsy's painting was her challenge.'' He paused. ''And possibly her escape.''

She'd never thought of it that way before, and her mouth pursed into a thoughtful line. ''You could be right about that. Still, if Mike were living I often wonder where we'd be today. Sooner or later he would have had to tell me about our financial situation.''

''I'm sure he would have, given time.'' Gray's eyes held hers. ''I've been thinking about what happened, and I don't think he was trying to bamboozle you. I think he was trying to protect you. He knew what you'd been through with your father and he didn't want you to worry. I'm sure he thought he'd have plenty of time to get things back on the right track. No one expects their life to end at thirty.''

"You could be right about that.'' And she imagined he was. It took some of the sting out of what she had perceived as Mike's betrayal for so long.

"Of course I could.'' He grinned when she narrowed her eyes at him. She walked her fingers over his ribs, and he gave a deep rumble of protest. "Hey! If you want to let your fingers do the walking, how about I show you the path?''

When she laughed, he caught her hand and splayed it flat on his abdomen, rubbing small circles. "Try that.''

She smiled, moving her free hand to open the button of his jeans, then slowly tugged down the zipper. "Okay. How about this?''

His only answer was a groan.

Her breath came faster as she burrowed her fingers beneath the elastic edge of his briefs, then slipped her hand inside and wrapped her fingers around him. Above her head Gray made an agonized sound. "You're killing me, sweet thing.''

He moved restlessly and the T-shirt on his chest fell aside.

And then she saw the scar. It was big. It was well-healed but clearly not ancient. "Dear Lord,'' she said, putting up a hand to trace the length of it. "Gray, I had no idea...''

But as she saw his face, her voice trailed off, and she knew. *She* knew.

Gray heaved himself upright, fastening his pants in one quick motion and yanking the discarded shirt over his head. "Catherine—"

"You have Mike's heart, don't you?" It was harsh and incredulous, and the words hung between them, demanding an answer.

"Yes," he said, his expression a study in guilt and anxiety. "I was going to tell you."

"When? After the wedding?" Her voice held a slightly hysterical edge.

"I didn't mean—"

"You already knew who I was when you introduced yourself to me, didn't you?" she demanded. *Don'tthinkdon'tthinkdon'tthink.*

He hesitated.

"Didn't you?"

"Yes.

"How did you find me?"

"I knew my donor was a young man from Baltimore. Mike's obituary was the only one that fit that profile on the right date." He took a deep breath. "You were in my head before we met. Your face, your voice—when I saw you, I knew right away who you were."

"Not possible." She backed away from him on her knees, afraid to try her legs for fear they wouldn't hold her.

He laughed, but there was no humor in it. "Don't you think that's what I thought?"

"You're lying," she said fiercely. "Someone

pointed me out to you. Does Patsy know or did you manipulate her, too?''

"Of course she doesn't know." He looked honestly shocked. He sighed and reached out a hand to her. "Catherine—"

"Don't touch me." Her teeth were chattering as the ugly truth sank in. "Don't ever touch me again." She managed to scramble to her feet and back toward the door. "I don't care if your house isn't finished, I want you to get out. Today."

"No," he said. "Not until you listen to me."

"Get out!" It was hoarse and ragged, beyond her control. "I'll call the hospital. I'll call the police, tell them you're harassing us." She fumbled for the doorknob, barely able to see for the tears that filled her eyes.

"I love you," he said. "You can't change that."

"You don't know what love is," she said bitterly. "You just want Mike's family and Mike's life. And Mike's wife."

He flinched, but his eyes didn't move from her face. "I *do* want you, Catherine. Not just now, but forever."

She shook her head, yanking open the door. "Never."

Later, she didn't remember the rush back to the house. But as she entered the kitchen, Patsy stood there making a cup of tea.

Her mother-in-law turned. "Michael's napping— what's wrong, dear?" A look of alarm crossing her face.

No! God, no, I can't tell her. But her heart sank as she realized that she was going to have to. "I just learned something that I didn't know about Gray before." She worked hard to keep her voice from cracking but it shook and she linked her fingers together, digging her fingernails into the backs of her hands. The small pain helped her focus. "Patsy…"

"What is it?" The older woman clutched at Catherine's hands.

Catherine turned her palms up. "Gray needed a heart transplant a couple of years ago. He—he received Mike's heart."

Patsy didn't react, and for a moment she wondered if the words had sunk in. Then Patsy's wrinkled face lit up with an incandescent joy Catherine wasn't sure she'd ever seen before, even when Michael was born. "Dear Lord," she whispered. "Thank you." She squeezed Catherine's hands so hard her grip hurt. "How utterly perfect! I've wanted so badly to meet the person who has my son's heart and here it turns out to be Gray—" She stopped suddenly, and her eyes widened. "Meeting us wasn't an accident, was it?" she asked, comprehension dawning.

Catherine shook her head, unable to speak.

"Oh, darling, I'm sure he had the best of motivations," Patsy said. "Even though it must seem as if he deliberately betrayed your trust."

"He did," Catherine said in a hard voice. "He lied by omission." *Just like Mike did when he didn't tell me the truth about our finances.*

"Oh, but…" Patsy's voice trailed off as she assessed the misery in Catherine's expression, the grim set of her mouth. "Give it some time," she finally suggested. "Don't do anything hasty."

"I don't," said Catherine, "intend to do anything at all." She turned and walked from the kitchen then, her throat aching with suppressed sobs that she knew were going to emerge any second.

She alternated between never wanting to see him again and wanting to smack him for deceiving her. The mere fact that she was angry enough to consider hitting someone was a shock—she had never been a violent person. She didn't like to allow herself to think too much about that morning, but bad dreams even invaded her sleep. She woke up with her jaw aching from grinding her teeth together while she slumbered.

You were in my head before we met. He'd meant it literally, she was certain. And she was flooded with memories of a dozen small incidents, recalling moments of unease at the way he'd seemingly read her mind.

He called Michael peanut—the day he fell. He knew my favorite flower, that I like butterscotch. He scratched my back. And on and on and on.

"How can that be?" It was an agonized whisper, heard only by the walls of her bedroom.

She wanted the whole thing never to have happened, wanted never to have seen that look—guilt mixed with fear—on his face. She wanted never to wonder if what he claimed was true. She wanted to go back to those perfect moments before his shirt had fallen aside.

But she couldn't.

Patsy had been to see him, she knew, although they hadn't discussed it. Her mother-in-law exuded a subtle glow of happiness that she couldn't completely dim even when trying to be subdued around Catherine.

And he still hadn't moved out.

She was too proud to ask Patsy about him. It had been eight days since she'd found out the truth, but she'd noticed his car still driving in and out the driveway and had seen lights on in the cottage. She'd asked him to leave. After what he'd done, he could have had the decency to grant her request.

So what did he do that was so terrible? He got your husband's heart—it isn't as if he had much of a choice. And if what he says about the memories is true, then he would have had to have been made of steel to resist looking you up.

He said he loves you. He wants to marry you. How terrible is that?

But it wasn't that easy, she thought angrily. And how did she know he was telling the truth? How did she know he hadn't just snooped around and found out a bunch of personal information?

She didn't.

But when she pulled her car into the garage after work on Wednesday, she got the chance to find out.

She parked in the big central bay. But as she stepped out of the car, the sunlight that streamed in through the open garage door was blocked. She turned, expecting Aline or Patsy—but it was a bigger, broad-shouldered form that filled the space.

"Catherine."

She stopped, unwilling to get any closer.

"I imagine you have some questions for me." His voice was quiet, neutral.

"Why haven't you left?" she said aggressively. "I asked you to leave."

"Not until we talk about this." His voice was inflexible. "I'll make you a deal. You come talk to me and afterward, I'll go."

"You're not exactly in a position to bargain."

"I am if you want to get rid of me."

"Oh, all right," she said, anger rising as hot and bitter as it had that first day. "Talk."

"Not here." He turned and walked away from the garage, halting at a small gazebo nearby.

Following, she took a seat on one of the stone benches. Despite the cauldron of feelings bubbling and roiling just beneath the surface of her emotions, a part of her noted the peaceful beauty of the shady little spot. Hostas spread their broad leaves along the path just outside, huge old oak trees kept the sun from invading at ground level, and astilbe and coral bells sent slender spears of color waving in the light breeze.

"What do you want to know?" He propped one foot on the end of the bench and rested his elbow on the bent knee.

"Nothing." She hoped her face was as stony as her voice. *Why did you need a heart transplant?*

When did you first begin to notice odd memories surfacing? What else do you recall—

"I can't believe you don't have any questions," he said conversationally.

"The night we met, you were shocked when I told you about my son. Because you didn't know." The words blurted themselves out without her permission, the only coherent thing to emerge from the mass of fragmented ideas swirling in her head.

Something flashed in his eyes. "'Shocked' is an understatement. I'd had you in my head for almost two years. But never a child."

"When did you first think something was unusual?"

He shrugged. "In the first couple of months after my transplant—" He shot her an apologetic look. "—I kept having dreams about a woman's face. Your face. And they weren't just dreams. You'd pop into my head at the most unexpected times. Later, I began to see you doing specific things—arranging flowers, in a long black evening dress, even coming toward me with a smile on your face…but it wasn't until my twenty-four-month checkup that it got more specific."

"What happened then?" She was interested despite herself.

"I saw a file notation about my donor heart coming from Johns Hopkins. So I got online and looked through the Baltimore paper because I knew the person probably had lived there, and I'd already been told it came from a young man who died in an accident. Mike was easy to find." He hesitated.

"What?"

"When I read your name in the obituary—" He raised blue eyes to her face and she could see the shock in them as if it had just happened. "—I knew as soon as I read your name that you were the woman."

"You assumed," she corrected.

"No." He shook his head. "I *knew*."

"And that's when you decided to invade our lives."

"No." His voice was calm, but she sensed that he was fighting the urge to shake her. "I only ever intended to look you up and watch you, see who you were and if you matched the face in my head. But after I saw you at that dance…" He shrugged. "I had to meet you."

"You could be lying." Her voice was shaking. "How do I know you didn't just hire someone to snoop through my life for little tidbits you could use?"

"If I'd done that, I'd have known about Michael," he pointed out.

His logic was irrefutable.

"It wasn't until after we met that I started to get a lot more specific information," he said.

"Such as?"

"Sweet thing. That's what he called you. I've never called a woman that before in my life." His voice sounded as strained as her nerves felt, and despite herself, she couldn't help thinking that if this *was* true and not just some crazy hoax, it couldn't have been easy for him. "Your favorite color is a dusky shade of rose. He told you he wanted to marry you in the kitchen at the party the night you met."

Dear God. He wasn't kidding. She'd never even told Patsy that. At the time, she'd laughed it off. It wasn't until months later when Mike asked her again that she even remembered he'd done it. She swallowed. "How...?"

"I saw it happen. You smiled and pretended he wasn't serious." He spread his hands when her mouth dropped open. "There's a theory—"

"Stop." She held up her hand, and a silence fell between them. "I need a minute."

"I know the feeling." His voice was very dry.

She let her hand drop and simply sat for a moment, her mind spinning. The implications of what he wanted her to believe were staggering. Another day in the garden slipped into her mind. "The first time you saw Michael..."

"I was overwhelmed." He swallowed. "I wasn't prepared for the way I felt when I saw him, proud and so happy—it was like *I* was his father."

"So explain it," she said abruptly. She wasn't ready to forgive him for lying to her—or at least, lying by omission—but she couldn't deny that his story was very convincing.

He shook his head. "I can't. There's a theory dealing with cellular memory that comes the closest. Very simply, it's believed that certain life experiences are actually imprinted in our cells. But even so, nothing as...detailed as what I've experienced has ever been recorded. Some transplantees report a craving for a certain kind of food that they never liked before, and it turns out to have been the favorite of the donor. Things like that are documented. But specific memories of prior events from the donor's life being transferred?'' He shook his head. ''I tried to talk about it once, but my doctors didn't seem to understand exactly how detailed my memories were. I was afraid they would think I'm crazy.''

She nodded. ''I bet.'' Then a new thought occurred to her. ''Have you told Patsy any of this?''

He looked horrified. ''Of course not.'' His expression eased as warmth seeped into his eyes. ''She's just happy to know that part of Mike is still living, in a sense, and especially pleased that she's been given the chance to get to know me.''

She felt her whole body sag in relief. ''Thank heavens.''

He took a deep breath. ''Mike must have loved you with every fiber of his being, because otherwise, why would I ever have known—''

''Exactly.'' She felt deflated, afraid to let herself accept what he offered. ''We wouldn't even have met if it hadn't been for this cellular memory, or whatever it is, that led you here.''

''You don't know that. Even without it, I might have been curious enough to try to locate my donor family, just to see you.'' He smiled crookedly, his eyes tender as they roamed her features. ''And I guarantee you that even without Mike's cells urging me on, I'd have been attracted to you.''

She hesitated. "What if your feelings for me are simply a product of receiving Mike's feelings with *his* heart?" She saw his eyes change as she spoke, and she realized that until that second he hadn't been sure she would ever forgive him. Neither had she, she acknowledged. Then she realized that much of her anger had dissipated during the previous revelations.

He didn't speak for a moment, and she felt ridiculously glad that he hadn't dismissed her concern. "No," he finally said. "If I were only experiencing Mike's memories, I would hate the idea of you working outside the home. But that doesn't bother me in the least."

"So...you're not feeling everything Mike did."

He shook his head. "I worried about that, too, at first. But now...I love you, Catherine. Me, Gray. You're just going to have to take it on faith, because I'll never be able to prove it to you. I'm going to need this heart for the rest of my life."

She swallowed. She wanted to throw herself into his arms, but...his words brought on a fresh fear. "How long...what kind of life span does a transplantee have?" She'd loved Mike and he died, but she knew that if she opened herself to what Gray was offering and then lost him as well, her heart would never recover.

"I have every hope of growing old with you, if you'll share your life with me," he said, his gaze warm and intense. "Transplantees are routinely living normal, productive lives now. There's a man in England still going strong after twenty-two years. You have to remember that many people who need transplants are either much older than I, or they have other significant medical conditions that complicate their life span prospects.'' He smiled again. ''I guess I'm a little bit of a guinea pig for my doctors. I was a normal, healthy young adult male, and I received a normal, healthy young adult heart that we all expect to keep working for a normal, healthy life span.''

''But what about rejection? Don't you risk getting sick?''

''I'll always have to take antirejection drugs and go to the hospital once or twice a year for checkups.'' His voice was patient, as if he'd been prepared for all her questions and concerns. ''But I'm on a very light dose of meds. I monitor myself carefully for signs of illness, try to eat well and avoid alcohol. I stay out of the sun because there's an increased risk of skin cancer, and I'm religious about my exercise program. Other than a few things I've incorporated into my lifestyle, Catherine, I am no different from any other man you've met.''

''Every other man doesn't have my husband's heart and memories,'' she pointed out, but she was smiling.

He straightened from the bench, coming forward and drawing her to her feet. ''I love you, Catherine. I'm sorry I didn't tell you right away who I was. I want to marry you and be a father to Michael, maybe give him some brothers and sisters one of these days. Will you consider it? You don't have to answer me now. I know this has been a lot to absorb—''

"Yes." She put a hand over his mouth. "Do you realize you babble when you're nervous?"

He nodded behind her hand, and then she felt his tongue whisk across her palm in a stealthy caress. "I love you," he mumbled. "Did that 'yes' mean yes, you'll consider it or—"

She removed her hand, smiling up at him. "I'll marry you."

"Whenever you like. I know how you feel about making this public too soon, and I'm sorry I reacted the way I did—"

"That reminds me," she said. "Patsy's big charity dance, the Iris Affair, is next Saturday night. Would you like to escort me?"

Gray's eyes closed for a second, and when they opened, they were glistening with moisture. It was clear that he recognized her olive branch. "I'd love to," he said. Then his hands slid down her back and drew her closer. As he dropped his head and sought her lips, he said, "So what are your plans for the rest of the afternoon?"

She slid her fingers up into his hair, slanting him a teasing smile. "Well…I'm a bit tired. Perhaps I could rest at your place for a little while. Then maybe later we could take Michael out for ice cream. What do you think?"

His fingers were already teasing open the buttons of her suit blouse. "Sounds like a plan."

The Iris Affair was probably the most beautiful event she'd ever attended, Catherine thought. Patsy was proud of her committee's efforts with good reason.

Crystal chandeliers sparkled overhead; on each table, irises in extraordinarily lovely hues floated in crystal bowls on each table. A large ice sculpture of an iris's delicate blossoms dominated a central table. Large arrangements of irises with other complementary flowers and greens decorated the buffet and the musicians' stage, and each female guest had received a single perfect iris which was pinned into her hair.

"I bet those people over there are talking about us." Gray's teasing tones floated down from above her head as they danced. "I think I heard the woman in the purple dress saying something about a hussy."

Catherine made a face as she thudded a fist against his solid arm. "You rat. I was terrified people would think I was after your money," she said.

Gray's chest heaved beneath her cheek and she felt him chuckle. "No one but us knows about your finances," he pointed out. "As far as the world knows, you're a wealthy young widow. Maybe they think I'm after your money."

"Fat chance," she said. "There are a few people who know the truth: my stockbroker, lawyer, and accountant."

"They're in no position to mention it to anyone," he reminded her. "Who would ever want to hire a professional who couldn't keep confidential information, confidential?"

"Speaking of confidential information," she said, "I had a doctor's appointment today and he says I should go off the Pill right away if we want to conceive within the next year.''

Gray's eyebrows rose and he smiled cautiously. "Is that what you want?"

She smiled up at him. "You're a part of this family in more ways than most people could ever imagine; I can't wait to have a baby that shares your genes."

His blue eyes shone, and he dropped a kiss on her temple as he pulled her into a close embrace that, if people weren't already talking, would surely set them to doing so. "I love you," he said in a deep, husky voice. "I will always be grateful to Mike for the gift of his heart and I promise you that as long as it beats in me, I will treasure you and Michael and any children we have together."

Catherine closed her eyes and rested her cheek against his shoulder, savoring the sweet words as they began to dance again. Her hand was caught close in his, resting right over the heart that had given both him *and* her a new chance at life.

* * * * *

*Don't miss Anne Marie Winston's
upcoming title*

BORN TO BE WILD,

part of Silhouette Desire's
Dynasties: The Barones,
in October 2003.

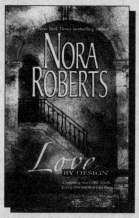

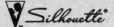

Is your man too good to be true?

Hot, gorgeous AND romantic?
If so, he could be a Harlequin® Blaze™ series cover model!

Our grand-prize winners will receive a trip for two to New York City to
shoot the cover of a Blaze novel, and will stay at the luxurious Plaza Hotel.
Plus, they'll receive $500 U.S. spending money!
The runner-up winners will receive $200 U.S.
to spend on a romantic dinner for two.

It's easy to enter!

In 100 words or less, tell us what makes your boyfriend or spouse a true romantic
and the perfect candidate for the cover of a Blaze novel, and include in your submission
two photos of this potential cover model.

All entries must include the written submission of the contest entrant, two photographs of the model
candidate and the Official Entry Form and Publicity Release forms completed in full and signed by
both the model candidate and the contest entrant. Harlequin, along with the experts at
Elite Model Management, will select a winner.

For photo and complete Contest details, please refer to the Official Rules on the next page. All entries
will become the property of Harlequin Enterprises Ltd. and are not returnable.

Please visit www.blazecovermodel.com to download a copy of the Official Entry Form and
Publicity Release Form or send a request to one of the addresses below.

Please mail your entry to: **Harlequin Blaze Cover Model Search**

In U.S.A.
P.O. Box 9069
Buffalo, NY
14269-9069

In Canada
P.O. Box 637
Fort Erie, ON
L2A 5X3

No purchase necessary. Contest open to Canadian and U.S. residents who are 18 and over.
Void where prohibited. Contest closes September 30, 2003.

HARLEQUIN® *Blaze*™

HBCVRMODEL1

HARLEQUIN BLAZE COVER MODEL SEARCH CONTEST 3569 OFFICIAL RULES
NO PURCHASE NECESSARY TO ENTER

1. To enter, submit two (2) 4" x 6" photographs of a boyfriend or spouse (who must be 18 years of age or older) taken no later than three (3) months from the time of entry: a close-up, waist up, shirtless photograph; and a fully clothed, full-length photograph, then, tell us, in 100 words or fewer, why he should be a Harlequin Blaze cover model and how he is romantic. Your complete "entry" must include: (i) your essay, (ii) the Official Entry Form and Publicity Release Form printed below completed and signed by you (as "Entrant"), (iii) the photographs (with your hand-written name, address and phone number, and your model's name, address and phone number on the back of each photograph), and (iv) the Publicity Release Form and Photograph Representation Form printed below completed and signed by your model (as "Model"), and should be sent via first-class mail to either: Harlequin Blaze Cover Model Search Contest 3569, P.O. Box 9069, Buffalo, NY, 14269-9069, or Harlequin Blaze Cover Model Search Contest 3569, P.O. Box 637, Fort Erie, Ontario L2A 5X3. All submissions must be in Canada and be received no later than September 30, 2003. Limit: one entry per person, household or organization. **Purchase or acceptance of a product offer does not improve your chances of winning.** All entry requirements must be strictly adhered to for eligibility and to ensure fairness among entries.

2. Ten (10) Finalist submissions (photographs and essays) will be selected by a panel of judges consisting of members of the Harlequin editorial, marketing and public relations staff, as well as a representative from Elite Model Management (Toronto) Inc., based on the following criteria:

Aptness/Appropriateness of submitted photographs for a Harlequin Blaze cover—70%

Originality of Essay—20%

Sincerity of Essay—10%

In the event of a tie, duplicate finalists will be selected. The photographs submitted by finalists will be posted on the Harlequin website no later than November 15, 2003 (at www.blazecovermodel.com), and viewers may vote, in rank order, on their favorite(s) to assist in the panel of judges' final determination of the Grand Prize and Runner-up winning entries based on the above judging criteria. All decisions of the judges are final.

3. All entries become the property of Harlequin Enterprises Ltd. and none will be returned. Any entry may be used for future promotional purposes. Elite Model Management (Toronto) Inc. and/or its partners, subsidiaries and affiliates operating as "Elite Model Management" will have access to all entries including all personal information, and may contact any Entrant and/or Model in its sole discretion for their own business purposes. Harlequin and Elite Model Management (Toronto) Inc. are separate entities with no legal association or partnership whatsoever having no power to bind or obligate the other or create any expressed or implied obligation or responsibility on behalf of the other, such that Harlequin shall not be responsible in any way for any acts or omissions of Elite Model Management (Toronto) Inc. or its partners, subsidiaries and affiliates in connection with the Contest or otherwise and Elite Model Management shall not be responsible in any way for any acts or omissions of Harlequin or its partners, subsidiaries and affiliates in connection with the contest or otherwise.

4. All Entrants and Models must be residents of the U.S. or Canada, be 18 years of age or older, and have no prior criminal convictions. The contest is not open to any Model that is a professional model and/or actor in any capacity at the time of the entry. Contest void wherever prohibited by law; all applicable laws and regulations apply. Any litigation within the Province of Quebec regarding the conduct or organization of a publicity contest may be submitted to the Régie des alcools, des courses et des jeux for a ruling, and any litigation regarding the awarding of a prize may be submitted to the Régie only for the purpose of helping the parties reach a settlement. Employees and immediate family members of Harlequin Enterprises Ltd., D.L. Blair, Inc., Elite Model Management (Toronto) Inc. and their parents, affiliates, subsidiaries and all other agencies, entities and persons connected with the use, marketing or conduct of this Contest are not eligible to enter. Acceptance of any prize offered constitutes permission to use Entrants' and Models' names, essay submissions, photographs or other likenesses for the purposes of advertising, trade, publication and promotion on behalf of Harlequin Enterprises Ltd., its parent, affiliates, subsidiaries, assigns and other authorized entities involved in the judging and promotion of the contest without further compensation to any Entrant or Model, unless prohibited by law.

5. Finalists will be determined no later than October 30, 2003. Prize Winners will be determined no later than January 31, 2004. Grand Prize Winners (consisting of winning Entrant and Model) will be required to sign and return Affidavit of Eligibility/Release of Liability and Model Release forms within thirty (30) days of notification. Non-compliance with this requirement and within the specified time period will result in disqualification and an alternate will be selected. Any prize notification returned as undeliverable will result in the awarding of the prize to an alternate set of winners. All travelers (or parent/legal guardian of a minor) must execute the Affidavit of Eligibility/Release of Liability prior to ticketing and must possess required travel documents (e.g. valid photo ID) where applicable. Travel dates specified by Sponsor but no later than May 30, 2004.

6. Prizes: One (1) Grand Prize—the opportunity for the Model to appear on the cover of a paperback book from the Harlequin Blaze series, and a 3 day/2 night trip for two (Entrant and Model) to New York, NY for the photo shoot of Model which includes round-trip coach air transportation from the commercial airport nearest the winning Entrant's home to New York, NY, (or, in lieu of air transportation, $100 cash payable to Entrant and Model, if the winning Entrant's home is within 250 miles of New York, NY), hotel accommodations (double occupancy) at the Plaza Hotel and $500 cash spending money payable to Entrant and Model, (approximate prize value: $8,000), and one (1) Runner-up Prize of $200 cash payable to Entrant and Model for a romantic dinner for two (approximate prize value: $200). Prizes are valued in U.S. currency. Prizes consist of only those items listed as part of the prize. No substitution of prize(s) permitted by winners. All prizes are awarded jointly to the Entrant and Model of the winning entries, and are not severable - prizes and obligations may not be assigned or transferred. Any change to the Entrant and/or Model of the winning entries will result in disqualification and an alternate will be selected. Taxes on prize are the sole responsibility of winners. Any and all expenses and/or items not specifically described as part of the prize are the sole responsibility of winners. Harlequin Enterprises Ltd. and D.L. Blair, Inc., their parents, affiliates, and subsidiaries are not responsible for errors in printing of Contest entries and/or game pieces. No responsibility is assumed for lost, stolen, late, illegible, incomplete, inaccurate, non-delivered, postage due or misdirected mail or entries. In the event of printing or other errors which may result in unintended prize values or duplication of prizes, all affected game pieces or entries shall be null and void.

7. Winners will be notified by mail. For winners' list (available after March 31, 2004), send a self-addressed, stamped envelope to: Harlequin Blaze Cover Model Search Contest 3569 Winners, P.O. Box 4200, Blair, NE 68009-4200, or refer to the Harlequin website (at www.blazecovermodel.com).

Contest sponsored by Harlequin Enterprises Ltd., P.O. Box 9042, Buffalo, NY 14269-9042.

HBCVRMODEL2

Silhouette

Desire

New York Times bestselling author

DIANA PALMER

MAN IN CONTROL

(Silhouette Desire #1537)

A brand-new

LONG, TALL Texans title.

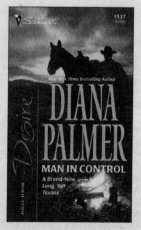

Eight years ago, DEA agent Alexander Cobb gave Jodie Clayburn a Texas-size brush-off. Now a covert investigation is making allies out of sworn enemies. When peril follows them home, can they remain in control? Tantalized to the core, this *Long, Tall Texan* would risk anything to protect—and possess—the woman he just can't resist.

Available October 2003 at your favorite retail outlet.

COMING NEXT MONTH

#1531 EXPECTING THE SHEIKH'S BABY—Kristi Gold
Dynasties: The Barones

The attraction between Sheikh Ashraf Ibn-Saalem and Karen Rawlins, the newest Barone, was white-hot. But Karen wanted control over her chaotic life—and a chance at motherhood. Ash offered to father her baby, but only as her husband. Dare Karen relinquish herself to Ash…body and soul?

#1532 FIVE BROTHERS AND A BABY—Peggy Moreland
The Tanners of Texas

Ace Tanner's deceased father had left behind a legacy of secrets— and a baby girl! Not daddy material, confirmed bachelor Ace hired Maggie Dean as a live-in nanny. But his seductive employee tempted him in ways he never expected. Could Ace be a family man after all?

#1533 A LITTLE DARE—Brenda Jackson

Shelly Brockman was the one who got away from Sheriff Dare Westmoreland. He was shocked to find her back in town and at his police station claiming the rebellious kid he had picked up—a kid he soon realized was his own….

#1534 SLEEPING WITH THE BOSS—Maureen Child

Rick Hawkins had been the bane of Eileen Ryan's existence. But now she was sharing close quarters with the handsome financial advisor as his fill-in secretary. She vowed to stay professional…but the sizzling chemistry between them had her *fantasies* working overtime.

#1535 IN BED WITH BEAUTY—Katherine Garbera
King of Hearts

Sexy restaurateur Sarah Malcolm found herself in a power struggle with Harris Davidson, the wealthy financier who threatened to take her business away. But their heated arguments gave way to heat of another kind…and soon she was sleeping with the enemy….

#1536 RULING PASSIONS—Laura Wright

Consumed by desire, Crown Prince Alex Thorne made love to the mysterious woman he had just rescued from the ocean. But when Sophia Dunhill ended up pregnant with his child he insisted she become his wife. Could his beautiful bride warm Alex's guarded heart as well as his bed?

SDCNM0803